THE

Cocktail

HOUR

Bar Keeps

Lenny's
Cocktail Lounge
ALSO VISIT
the HUT | DEL REY Club
UNSURPASSED
for
FINE DRINKS

Casa Orinda
ENJOY A GLIMPSE OF THE EARLY WEST
DINE | DANC
ORINDA CROSS ROADS
ORINDA, CALIF.
ORINDA 9811

Bourb

Dantes
COCKTAILS

CHARCOAL BROILED STEAKS • COCKTAILS
the **Palms**
DANCING
Dance to
'NAME' BANDS
SAN GABRIEL VALLEY
Dancing Center
ON HIGHWAY 66
Glendora

Bar Keeps

A COLLECTION OF CALIFORNIA's BEST

cocktail Napkins

PATRICK QUINN

DESIGN BY **J. ERIC LYNXWILER**

A Votre Santé
NA ZDROVÉ!
OOGIE WAWA!
Here's How!
SKOL!
SALUD!
PROSIT!
cheerio!
DOBRE ZDROWIE

Contents

The Cocktail Crowd

Those with nothing else to do

The Commuters

The Beer Crowd

Introduction
A Century of Alcohol in America

In the summer of 1943, famed lyricist Johnny Mercer sat at the bar in P.J. Clarke's on 3rd Avenue in Manhattan. Over the course of a few drinks, he came up with the lyrics to the classic torch song *One for My Baby (And One More for the Road)*. Mercer scribbled the words on a cocktail napkin to show his musical cohort, composer Harold Arlen. A few months later, Fred Astaire was singing the tune in the musical comedy *The Sky's the Limit*.

But, fast-forward to the spring of 1958. Frank Sinatra recorded the song in the Capitol Records studios at Hollywood and Vine. It was the key track on his album, *Frank Sinatra Sings for Only the Lonely*. His version soon became the last-call soundtrack on every jukebox across the country.

World War II ended in 1945, and millions of soldiers returned from Europe and the Pacific. They left as boys and returned as men: young Americans who had seen the world, experienced other cultures, and felt Death's cold breath on the back of their necks. These combat-weary veterans needed some release. They wanted to drink, dance, and have a good time—maybe even meet a nice girl who'd slip them a phone number scribbled on the back of a cocktail napkin. Just a humble square of white paper—but now, it was gold.

Now those vets had a G.I. Bill in one hand, and a cold beer in the other. They were ready to get married, buy homes, raise families, and settle down. In 1946 alone, more than three million babies were delivered in the United States.

The government subsidized low-cost mortgages for returning soldiers, which meant that it was often cheaper to buy a place in the suburbs than to rent an apartment in the city. Land developers saw an opportunity and began building new communities across the country. Instant neighborhoods filled with inexpensive tract houses. Model homes came with a yard in front and a patio out back. These suburban developments were built on the outskirts of major cities, in areas with few conveniently located businesses. Only the highway connected them to the world.

For decades, taverns and saloons had been dark caves filled with middle-aged men smoking Old Golds and drinking Rainier Ale. But suburban expansion led not just to societal shifts, but also to the emergence of hotel and restaurant bars that offered quality food, a jukebox to dance to, and where, most importantly, everyone was welcome to join the party.

And party they did. The folks that newsman Tom Brokaw would later call the Greatest Generation—men and women alike—hit their neighborhood watering holes ready to drink concoctions with names like sloe gin fizz, whiskey sour, Havana cooler, and Singapore sling. And every drink was served with its own four-by-four-inch cocktail napkin, emblazoned with a message, a cartoon, or a logo to reflect the mood of the bar that served up the spirits.

Those cocktail napkins were just part of a Saturday night out at the local watering holes. And the messages printed on them were a reflection of the times. Excessive drinking, smoking, sexism, adultery—even racism—were once thought of as humorous, no matter how base and distasteful. Labels like "Not PC" and "Designated Driver" didn't exist in the 1940s and '50s.

New suburban cocktail lounges were designed to appeal to a younger crowd: men and women who were ready to blow off some steam and cut a rug. Or couples who'd hired a babysitter and were desperate to get out of the house for a night on the town. Sometimes, a husband or wife showed up alone, his or her wedding ring slipped into a side pocket for the night. And it was as if the cartoons on the cocktail napkins endorsed—or, at least, predicted—these "extracurricular" activities.

By the mid-1950s, Americans were on the road. The Federal-Aid Highway Act of 1956 funded 41,000 miles of the Interstate Highway System. More than any other destination, California was calling. Hollywood, Disneyland, the Golden Gate, Yosemite, Sequoia—California had it all to offer. Newlyweds in convertibles and nuclear families in Airstream trailers got their kicks on Route 66. It seemed that every Main Street in America that wound through the Midwest headed straight for California—hundreds of miles lined by cafes, motels, restaurants, and cocktail lounges. Crossing into California, options included the likes of **Red Rooster Cafe** in Victorville, **The Oasis** in Redlands, **Three O Two** bar in Santa Ana, **Stardust Room** in Long Beach, and **Moby's Dock** on Santa Monica Pier, **Hilo Club** in Atherton, or **Ed Hogarty's Berkeley Square Cocktail Lounge**.

As the 1950s turned to the 1960s, ambiance was no longer a dirty word when it came to cocktail spots. Tiki bars took patrons on a trip to the South Seas with bandleader Martin Denny as their tour guide. Western-themed roadhouses, exotic Chinese lounges, and south-of-the-border cantinas provided an escape, no matter what part of the country drinkers called home. Regardless of the weather, you could always get a mai tai at the Crow's Nest, a zombie punch at the **Hilo Club**, or a margarita at the **Oasis** in Redlands. Their cocktail napkins featured Kahuna totems, laughing Buddhas, and crooning mariachi singers. All sure-fire guarantees of a good time.

These are cocktail lounges that have come and gone, razed by the bulldozer of progress. This collection is a way to reconnect with that time and take that journey. So why not pull off the highway and park the convertible out back. Walk in the door, drop a quarter in the juke, and order an old fashioned; pretend it's Saturday night.

Warning: some of the napkins in this book walk a very fine line between ironic, funny, and totally offensive. But regard them as ephemeral artifacts from the past; rare cocktail napkin history.

TOM COLLINS
SIDE CAR • MANHATTAN
PLANTERS PUNCH • JACK ROSE
MARTINI • RUM SWIZZLE • DAIQUIRI
WHISKEY SOUR • BACARDI • GIN BUCK
CUBA LIBRE
ALEXANDER
HAVANA COOLER
GIN FIZZ • BRONX
SCOTCH & SODA
GIN RICKEY
MINT JULEP
SINGAPORE SLING
OLD FASHIONED
OE GIN FIZZ
WOT'LL IT BE ?

A History of Cocktail Napkins

Napkins date back to the ancient Greeks who used lumps of bread dough called *apomagdalie* to tidy their fingers after a meal. The Romans were the first to use a cloth napkin or *sudarium*. In medieval times, royal banquets included a court *ewerer* who carried a towel for guests to wipe their hands. In the eighteenth century, the French court imposed strict rules on the of use napkins: one 1729 treatise stated, "It is ungentlemanly to use a napkin for wiping the face or scraping the teeth, and a most vulgar error to wipe one's nose with it." Still sage advice.

COCKTAILS

Elbow Room

FONTANA   CALIFORNIA

HOW TO LIVE ON $15 A WEEK

WHISKEY AND BEER	$ 8.80
WIFE'S BEER	1.65
MEAT, FISH AND GROCERIES, ON CREDIT	
RENT	PAY NEXT WEEK
MID-WEEK WHISKEY	1.50
COAL	BORROW NEIGHBORS
LIFE INSURANCE (WIFE'S)	
CIGARS	.50
MOVIES	.20
PINOCHLE CLUB	.60
HOT TIP ON HORSES	.50
DOG FOOD	.50
SNUFF	.60
POKER GAME	.40
	1.40
	$16.65

**THIS MEANS GOING IN DEBT
SO CUT OUT THE WIFE'S BEER**

Cocktails & Bartenders

In the 1940s, there was no such thing as a "mixologist" and certainly no "craft cocktails." Bartenders were variations of Nick, the guy who ran the bar for Mr. Martini in *It's A Wonderful Life*. Depending on the joint, he might resemble Nick before Jimmy Stewart tried to kill himself: a stand-up fella who'd offer to find you a ride home when you were down on your luck. But then there was also Nick after Jimmy jumps off the bridge. That Nick is there to serve hard drinks to men who want to get drunk fast, and he doesn't need characters around to give the joint "atmosphere."

But society's views on the tenders of bars have changed. When the Iceman cometh, now he goes to his version of *Cheers*, where everybody knows his name. Every pub or tavern should have a Sam and Woody greeting folks from behind the bar. And with luck, Isaac from *The Love Boat* has the weekend shift, not Lloyd from *The Shining*. Ironically, the bartender most people are familiar with only knows how to pour one drink, Duff Beer. Moe from *The Simpsons* and Nick would have gotten along famously.

No one is quite sure how—or where—the term "cocktail" came into being, but there are some interesting theories. As one debunked but very popular story goes, Antoine Amédée Peychaud escaped the French Revolution in the mid-1880s and relocated to New Orleans. He was known to mix his own recipe for bitters with brandy into a remedy for stomach ailments, and served it in an egg cup. In French, the egg cup is called a *coquetier*. That term morphed into "cocktay" and eventually "cocktail." However, we must point out that the term "cocktail" surfaced in about 1803, the same year Peychaud was born, according to one of his descendants. That would mean he was mixing bitters and brandy in an egg cup before he could talk, *if* we are to believe this particular legend.

GREEN SPOT
VICTORVILLE, CALIF.
COCKTAIL LOUNGE

Cocktails
Mountain Way Club
40th AND SIERRA WAY
SAN BERNARDINO

DAIQUIRI

OLD FASHIONED

MARTINI

MANHATTAN

Name it, Brother

Another story set during the American Revolution tells of an innkeeper who served a meal to some French soldiers. To show her appreciation for their support of colonial troops, she decorated their drinks with feathers from a neighbor's rooster. The soldiers supposedly cheered "*Vive le cock-tail.*" Pick your legend; there are plenty more where these came from.

One thing the history books do agree upon is that the concept of a bartender as someone who makes a drink—rather than someone who merely pours one—started with Jerry Thomas. Nicknamed "The Professor," he published the first ever bartending guide called *The Bon Vivant's Companion* in 1862. His biggest claim to fame is the creation of the martini, though he called his version a "martinez" and included a dash of maraschino liqueur.

The Eighteenth Amendment to the U.S. Constitution, ratified in 1917, established Prohibition, which turned the liquor industry upside down when it went into effect in 1920. Public bars became private speakeasies that were run by mobsters and corrupt officials. They served bootlegged alcohol either brought in from Canada or brewed up in basement distilleries. At best, this homemade hooch would simply be watered-down whiskey or rum. At worst, it was pure wood-grain alcohol mixed with ginger ale or Coca-Cola to hide the harsh taste. There were even rumors of bootleggers adding rotted meat or a few dead rats to give it a bourbon flavor.

Prohibition was finally repealed in 1933, but the party didn't last long. American entered World War II and most men took Nick's advice. They stuck with hard drinks so they could get drunk fast. The war ended in 1945 and things had changed. Americans now celebrated with mai tais at Trader Vic's or zombies at Don the Beachcomber. It wasn't until 1962, when Sean Connery made his first appearance as James Bond in *Dr. No.* that suddenly, the entire nation wanted their vodka martinis shaken, not stirred.

OBIES

CRESTLINE SAN BERNARDINO MOUNTAINS

4800 FEET HIGH—A GOOD PLACE TO GET HIGHER

PHONE—6187

14

Specialty cocktails pretty much took a backseat for the next generation; Baby Boomers (who hadn't been called that yet) were too busy making their moves at the Regal Beagle to worry about choosing between a rusty nail or a pink lady. The 1980s saw the unfortunate popularity of themed restaurant chains such as the Hard Rock Café, TGI Friday's, and Planet Hollywood. Throw in the popularity of Tom Cruise starring behind the bar in the film *Cocktail*, and bartenders finally got more than their fifteen minutes of fame. It wasn't good enough that your local bartender knew how to make a Fuzzy Navel or a Sex on the Beach. They had to be able to do it with flair. This was also the same period that saw the popularity of drinks like the Slippery Nipple and Slow Comfortable Screw Up Against the Wall. So needless to say, the subtlety of a well-made Negroni wasn't on anyone's radar.

Moving into the 1990s, vodka continued to dominate the bar scene when a Swedish company introduced the concept of flavored vodka. Cocktails like the Lemon Drop and the cosmopolitan were the 'It' drinks of the '90s. The Cosmo, official drink of Carrie Bradshaw and friends on *Sex and the City*, was created by bartender Toby Cecchini at the Odeon in Tribeca. Across town, Dale Degroff was reinventing classic cocktails at the Rainbow Room in Rockefeller Center. This was the beginning of the Mixology Movement.

Which leads us to the question, what's the difference between a bartender and a mixologist? The easy answer is a bartender follows existing recipes and a mixologist creates new ones. But that would be an insult to bartenders. Any schmuck with a liquor cabinet can pour a Manhattan. A good bartender chooses the best liquor and pours the exact amounts to create the perfect drink. Because when it's one in the morning and Sinatra's playing on the jukebox, only perfect will do.

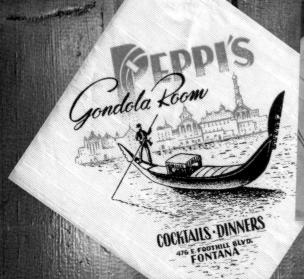

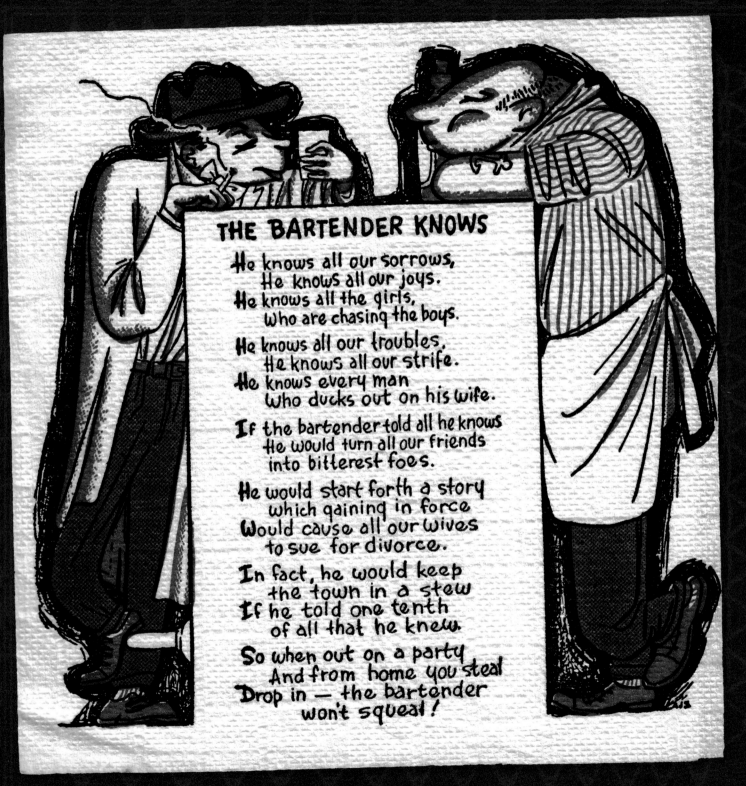

A History of Cocktail Napkins

The invention of paper is generally credited to Cai Lun, a Chinese court official of the Eastern Han Dynasty, sometime around 105 CE. The earliest version of the paper napkin was recorded centuries later in 610 CE during the Tang Dynasty, when the Chinese used small pieces of paper folded into squares known as *chich pha* to hold their tea cups. Around that same time, a Korean Buddhist priest called Damjing introduced the Japanese to the art of making paper, who then used *kozo* (mulberry) and hemp fibers for strength. By the 1800s, Japanese paper was regarded as the finest in the world.

Hollywood

DRINKING IN HISTORY

In the 1930s, Hollywood was known as the Dream Factory, the kind of place where people in the rest of the country liked to think that actors like Lana Turner could be discovered sipping a soda at the counter of Schwab's drugstore. They didn't really care that she was actually first spotted at the Top Hat Café across the street from Hollywood High.

Hollywood was also a never-ending party. Celebrities packed the dance floors of Hollywood's most popular nightclubs. Frank Senne's Moulin Rouge, the Hollywood Palladium, Bob Brooks' 7 Seas, Florentine Gardens, the Latin Quarter—the list went on and on. Further west on the Sunset Strip, there was always a crowd at Ciro's, Mocambo, Café Trocadero, and the bar at the Chateau Marmont Hotel.

A few of those places are still around and still attract the occasional celebrity: Formosa Café, which opened in 1925; El Coyote, where the bartenders mixed its first margarita in 1931. Originally a speakeasy connected to the Pantages Theatre during Prohibition, the Frolic Room opened as a legal bar in 1934. The waiters have been singing show tunes at Miceli's since 1949. And in 2019, Musso & Frank Grill celebrated a century of serving the best martini in town.

The
HANGOVER
1456 NORTH VINE STREET
HOLLYWOOD

Latin
Quarter
5521 SUNSET BLVD.
HOLLYWOOD
PH · HO · 93445

and
LUCKY
SPOT
CAFE
Polly   Alex
1107
N. WESTERN AVE.
Hollywood Calif.
HE. 3903

HOTEL
KNICKERBOCKER

the FOG CUTTERS' cafe

Featuring The Famous
Fog Cutter
1635 NORTH LA BREA
AT HOLLYWOOD BLVD.
HO. 9698

THE TEMPLE OF
HEAVENLY "SPIRITS"
THE JADE
ON THE BOULEVARD IN HOLLYWOOD · INTERESTING SURROUNDINGS
DELICIOUS COCKTAILS · TASTY FOODS

Ciro's
HOLLYWOOD
H. D. HOVER presents
AMERICA'S FOREMOST
ATTRACTIONS

The Circle

2937 OCEAN FRONT
OCEAN PARK
·
HOLLYWOOD BLVD. AT McCADDEN
HOLLYWOOD

Gourmet

6530
Sunset Blvd.

One of Hollywood's first major nightspots was the Café Montmartre. Adolph "Eddie" Brandstatter, who had worked in Paris and London before coming to Los Angeles, owned the place, and even though Prohibition was still in full swing, Eddie always made sure there was a bootlegger on the premises to keep his customers happy. Another highlight was its Charleston contest held every Tuesday night. Winners included "It Girl" Clara Bow and a then-unknown actress named Joan Crawford. After one-too-many bad business decisions, Eddie sold the club and declared bankruptcy.

In 1933, Eddie opened **Sardi's**, an Art Deco palace that quickly became one of Hollywood's sizzling hotspots. But three years later, a fire nearly destroyed it. When Sardi's reopened, its former luster was gone. Eddie tried to bounce back with a new restaurant, the Bohemian Grill. But it was just one of ten different nightclubs he opened over the course of the next twenty years. Failure upon failure apparently was too much for him, and he committed suicide in 1940.

In 1941, local radio personality Tom Breneman began a live broadcast from Sardi's called Breakfast

at Sardi's, that morphed into Breakfast in Hollywood. The show proved to be so popular, Breneman bought the Hollywood Recreation Center, a bowling alley on North Vine Street. He converted the bowl into his own restaurant—Tom Breneman's—and started broadcasting his show from there.

Sardi's was sold in the late 1940s and became the Chi-Chi Club, part of a small chain of tiki bars based in Palm Springs. That lasted only a few years; in 1953, new owners Sam Donata and Ben Arkin renamed it **Zardi's Jazzland**. They kept the Polynesian decor, but the main draw was jazz: Dave Brubeck, Ella Fitzgerald, Chet Baker, Billie Holiday, and Oscar Peterson—the best of the best. The club was so cool that it attracted Marlon Brando as a regular.

But even Zardi's Jazzland closed in 1959. A few years later, the venue became the Haunted House, a dance club that featured a giant monster's head with a stage for live bands in its mouth. As guests first entered, they walked through a dark cave filled with horror-movie waxworks including Frankenstein and Dracula. Like Sardi's and Zardi's Jazzland before it, the Haunted House was popular with celebrities, but now the likes of Sonny and Cher and comedian Phyllis Diller were on the dance floor.

As the 1960s came to an end, so did the Haunted House. By 1971, Hollywood Boulevard had begun to look a little seedier, more like New York's Times Square. The club re-opened its doors as The Cave, a pornographic bookstore and movie house. The stage also had a comeback when the name changed to Hollywood Cabaret Strip Club. But by 2019, the club that saw Ella sing the standards and Sonny and Cher dance the Frug was empty and abandoned, waiting for its next incarnation.

FRANK SENNE'S MOULIN ROUGE

Earl Carroll Theatre opened in 1938, built at an estimated cost of a half-million dollars. The glamorous thousand-seat supper club featured a sixty-foot-wide revolving stage. Its Sunset Boulevard façade featured a twenty-four-foot neon outline of the face of Carroll's girlfriend, Beryl Wallace, one of the club's dancers, and around her head like a halo were the words: "Thru these portals pass the most beautiful girls in the world." The club was such a sensation that Paramount released the musical *A Night at Earl Carroll's*. But tragedy struck in 1948 when Carroll and Wallace died in a plane crash.

Frank Senne took over the venue, renamed it **Moulin Rouge**, and opened the doors on Christmas Day 1953. It soon became the hottest nightclub in America, featuring performers such as Louis Armstrong and Peggy Lee. It also became home to the daytime television show *Queen for a Day*. But in the late 1950s, Frank sold the club and moved to Las Vegas.

After a short stint as a go-go club called Hullabaloo, the venue became the Aquarius Theater in 1968; it took its name to highlight the West Coast production of *Hair*, the show that ran continuously for two years. Cast members included Ben Vereen, Jennifer Warnes, and Meat Loaf, years before he appeared in the original L.A. production of *Rocky Horror Picture Show*.

In 1978, Center Theatre Group used the venue to stage the extended run of its blockbuster play *Zoot Suit*, starring Edward James Olmos. In 1983, the theater became home to the TV show *Star Search*, hosted by Ed McMahon, that ran until 1995. Nickelodeon leased the space as its West Coast production center from 1997 until 2016.

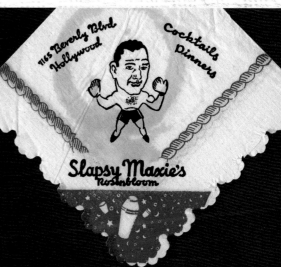

Max Rosenbloom was a professional boxer who earned the nickname "Slapsie Maxie" for his unusual style of fighting. When he retired in 1934, he began a second career as a part-time actor and full-time night-club owner. His first **Slapsy Maxie's** opened on Beverly Boulevard in a former burlesque theater, but in 1943, the club moved to Wilshire Boulevard. For years the new space had been home to the **Wilshire Bowl**, a popular nightspot that booked acts such as Dean Martin and Jerry Lewis. The new club was also a front for mobster Mickey Cohen, who ran his bookmaking operations on the second floor. Cohen went to prison for tax evasion in 1951, and Slapsy Maxie's became the Mardi Gras. Eventually, the building was destroyed and a Van De Kamp's coffee shop was built on the property. In the 1960s, the club's original location on Beverly Boulevard was converted into a movie theater. It first opened as the Europa, showing foreign films, and then as Eros, screening adult films, which closed in 1977. When new owners took over, they called it the New Beverly Cinema, which opened on May 5, 1978, screening a Marlon Brando double feature of *A Streetcar Named Desire* and *Last Tango in Paris*. Nearly thirty years later, director Quentin Tarantino renovated the place and continued showing film classics.

THE BROWN DERBY

During the 1920s, Programmatic architecture was all the rage. Stores or restaurants were built in shapes meant to promote their product. Some examples still exist, like the massive doughnut on the roof of Randy's Donuts in Inglewood or the restored Idle Hour, a bar inside what looks like a giant wine barrel. But perhaps the most iconic example of Programmatic architecture is the original **Brown Derby**, opened in 1926 on Wilshire Boulevard. Shaped like a hat, it quickly became a magnet for the Hollywood set, and, of course, tourists.

A second Brown Derby opened in 1929 near the corner of Hollywood and Vine. Though not shaped like a hat, it was an immediate success with actors who were working on films being shot at the nearby studios. In 1954, Lucille Ball filmed an episode of *I Love Lucy* on a set that replicated the Derby. A third restaurant opened in Beverly Hills in 1931. Also located on Wilshire Boulevard, across from the Beverly Wilshire Hotel, it was the last Brown Derby to close—in 1982.

Another branch of the chain was on Los Feliz Boulevard near Griffith Park. Initially a fried chicken restaurant called **Willard's**, the menu proudly declared "This is the house that serves the chickens whose feet never touch the ground." In 1940, director Cecil B. DeMille bought the property and invested in what would become yet another Brown Derby.

Almost as popular as the restaurants was the drink of the same name. The Brown Derby is made with two parts whiskey, one part grapefruit juice, and one part honey, all poured over cracked ice, shaken well, and strained into a cocktail glass. Ironically, the drink wasn't invented at the Brown Derby. One origin story says a bartender at the Vendome Club on the Sunset Strip concocted it, but another version has the drink born in New York City, using rum and maple syrup instead of whiskey and honey.

California Hotels

A hotel can mean different things to different people. It can be a place to spend the night after a long day of travel. An escape from the mundane daily routine. A rendezvous spot to meet with friends or loved ones (or in some cases, an illicit rendezvous, depending on who's meeting up). So when a hotel is in business for over 160 years, it must be doing something right. California's first hotel, the National in the Gold Rush town of Jamestown, opened in 1859, and it's still going strong. But there are many others of note.

HOLLYWOOD PLAZA HOTEL

Hollywood Plaza Hotel opened its doors in 1925 on Vine Street just a few doors south of Hollywood Boulevard. Costing more than a million dollars, it was one of the most luxurious hotels in the city, with a smoking lounge for men and a garden patio filled with date palms. In 1928, the Pig'n Whistle restaurant chain took over the café. Then it became the Russian Eagle Café in 1931, where guests dined to the strains of Romani songs. Five years later, a swank nightclub called the Cinnabar moved in, only to be replaced with the It Café. Actor Rex Bell gave It to his wife Clara "It Girl" Bow, after she retired from the silent screen. Two weeks after it opened, Bow learned she was pregnant, and the restaurant closed. The cafe soon became Les Comiques, and then The Westerner Lounge & Grill. The hotel only attracted tourists and, like Hollywood Boulevard, was showing its age. In 1973, the whole place was converted to senior housing and never looked back.

HOLLYWOOD ROOSEVELT HOTEL

On May 15, 1927, the **Hollywood Roosevelt Hotel** opened on Hollywood Boulevard across the street from Sid Grauman's Chinese Theatre. Construction of the hotel cost 2.5 million dollars, and was financed by a group that included Louis B. Mayer, Mary Pickford, and Douglas Fairbanks. The first Academy Awards ceremony took place in the hotel's Blossom Ballroom, even though the winners had been announced three months before. The entire ceremony lasted just fifteen minutes, with Fairbanks handing out the awards. In 1936, the hotel added a popular jazz club, the **Cinegrill**.

Guests and tourists are drawn to the hotel by its vintage décor and because it's reportedly one of the most haunted places in town. And two ghosts are its star attractions.

Marilyn Monroe called Room 1200 home for two years during the 1940s, and even shot her first magazine cover by the hotel's pool. Not long after her passing, guests and employees said they caught glimpses of a sad blonde in the room's full-length mirror. Coincidentally, Marilyn's ghost has also been "seen" numerous times at the Hotel Knickerbocker.

Montgomery Clift, the famed Method actor, stayed in Room 928 for three months in 1952, while filming *From Here to Eternity*. Four years later, he barely survived a terrible car accident, and was in constant pain that he tried to overcome with prescription painkillers and alcohol. On July 22, 1966, he was found dead in his bathtub from a heart attack at the age of forty-five. Since then, guests staying in Room 928 say they have awakened to find him pacing the foyer. Others say they have heard him practicing his trumpet. Guests say they have felt him brush up against them.

HOLLYWOOD-ROOSEVELT HOTEL

27

THE AMBASSADOR

The Ambassador opened at the stroke of midnight on January 1, 1921. The hotel's nightclub, the Cocoanut Grove, featured papier-maché coconut trees with stuffed monkeys swinging from their branches, and its ceiling was painted like a starry night sky. Celebrities from Mary Pickford to Howard Hughes danced to the sounds of Freddy Martin and his orchestra. June 5, 1968 put The Ambassador in the history books forever, though. After he made a victory speech in its Embassy Ballroom, Senator Robert F. Kennedy took a shortcut through the hotel's kitchen, where he was shot to death by Sirhan Sirhan. The hotel finally closed in 1989 and was later demolished, but the property is now the site of six school campuses known as the Robert F. Kennedy Community Schools.

BILTMORE
LOS ANGELES

Biltmore Manhattan (a Colossal Cocktail) 25

GRILL · DINNER
A LA CARTE
September 7, 1942

THE GRILL IS OPEN SUNDAY

FREE PARKING Next Door in P. M. Garage
after 6 p.m. and All Day Sunday
Ask the Waiter to Validate Your Parking Ticket

BILTMORE SPECIAL DINNER
Served from Noon till 9:00 p.m.

SELECTION OF ENTREE INDICATES PRICE OF DINNER

Please do not Substitute on this Menu

Prawn, Shrimp or Crab Meat Cocktail 70	Olympia Oyster Cocktail 75
Smoked Salmon 65	Canape of Domestic Caviar 1.50
Hearts of Sacramento Celery 40	Fruit Supreme 50
Giblet Broth, English Style 25	Vegetable Soup, Cultivateur 25
Onion Soup au Gratin 50	
Today's Jellied Broth: Consomme or Tomato 30	

Sauce 70

...burg W...

BILTMORE HOTEL

When the **Biltmore Hotel** opened in 1923, it was the largest hotel west of Chicago. Legend has it that the idea for the Academy Awards was devised over drinks in the hotel's Crystal Ballroom. Louis B. Mayer, who ran MGM Studios, came up with the idea, half-jokingly suggesting that people in the industry should be recognized for their artistic merit rather than financial success. Also sitting at the table was art director Cedric Gibbons, who sketched a statuette on a cocktail napkin. That sketch evolved into the Oscar that is presented annually at the Academy Awards ceremony.

Perhaps the Biltmore's most famous legacy is being the last place that Elizabeth Short, known more commonly as the Black Dahlia, was seen alive. Her ghost is said to still wander the tenth and eleventh floors. In her honor, the hotel's Gallery Bar offers a Black Dahlia cocktail, a mix of citrus vodka, Chambord, and Kahlua.

HOTEL KNICKERBOCKER

Hotel Knickerbocker, which opened in 1929 and closed in 1973, had a knack for winding up in gossip columns. For instance, on Halloween night in 1936, Bess Houdini, the widow of magician Harry Houdini, held a séance on the hotel roof. Harry's ghost never showed, but the headlines were big.

On July 23, 1948, filmmaker D.W. Griffith died of a cerebral hemorrhage after being discovered unconscious in the hotel lobby. During the last year of his life, he lived alone in a room at the Knickerbocker. A poignant final act for the man who had once been called the world's greatest film director.

In 1962, celebrated costume designer Irene Lentz checked into a room on the eleventh floor. Devastated by her husband's recent stroke and the death of her lover, Gary Cooper, Lentz got drunk and penned multiple suicide notes. One written to the other hotel guests read like this: "Sorry I had to drink so much to get the courage to do this." She then slit her wrists. Still not dead by 3:20 p.m., she jumped to her death from a hotel window.

HOTEL CLAREMONT

In 1904, Frank Havens won 13,000 acres of land in a game of checkers. He decided to build the largest hotel on the west coast on prime real estate that overlooked San Francisco Bay. Construction was interrupted by the 1906 San Francisco Earthquake, so the Hotel Claremont didn't open until 1915.

In 1937, after new owner Claude Gillum expanded the Claremont, state officials decreed it was too close to UC Berkeley to qualify for a liquor license. But a coed measured carefully, discovering that the hotel's front steps were a few feet more than a mile from the college. The license was granted, and the coed was awarded free drinks at the hotel for the rest of her life.

Opened in 1925, the six-story **Antlers Hotel** was San Bernardino's first skyscraper. Besides its lobby decorated with mounted animal heads, all displaying dramatic antlers, the hotel's other claim to fame was its "fireproof" construction. Built with steel-reinforced concrete, the only wood in the building was found in the door jambs. Even the furniture in the rooms was steel-frame construction. The owners were so proud of the work, they hung a large sign on the side of the building that read "Antlers Hotel, Absolutely Fireproof."

In the 1920s, daredevils were all the rage. Whether dancing on the wing of a flying plane, tightrope-walking between tall buildings, or rolling over Niagara Falls in a wooden barrel, these fearless folks never ceased to amaze. J.J. Woods was famous for performing as the Human Fly. He would scale the sides of skyscrapers with no trace of safety rigs. When he decided to climb atop Antlers Hotel, he added a unique spin to his act. He walked around the edge of the hotel roof, balancing his wife on one shoulder and his young daughter on the other—blindfolded.

Eventually all Human Fly acts fell out of favor after one-too-many performers tumbled to their deaths, occasionally injuring or killing bystanders on the street below. By the late 1950s, with no Woods to attract guests, Antlers Hotel also fell out of favor, and it was torn down in January 1961.

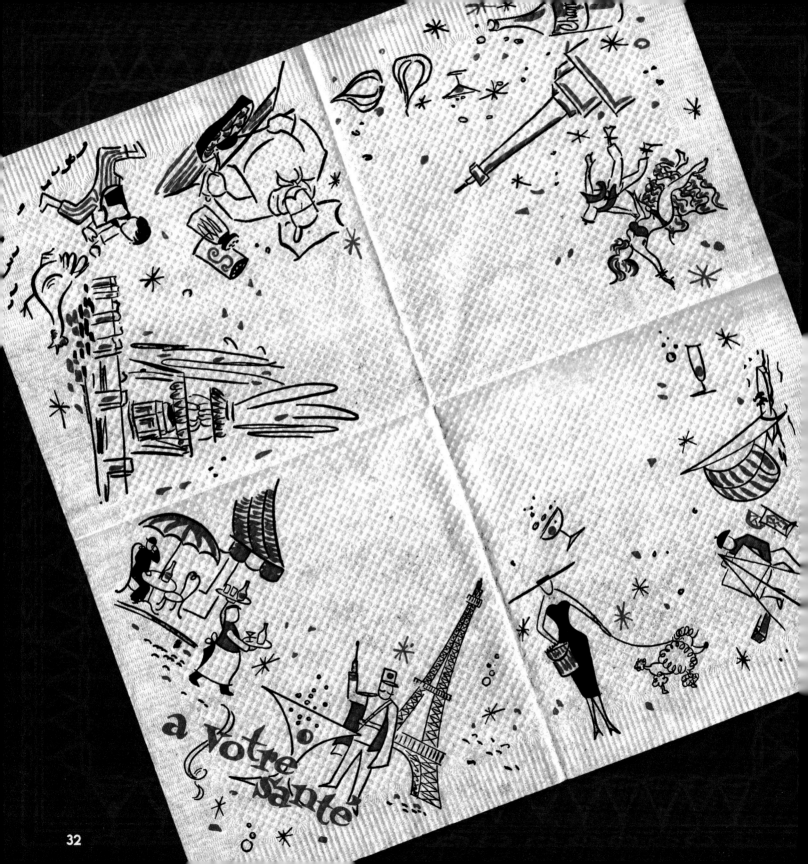

A History of Cocktail Napkins

In 1887, the British firm John Dickinson Ltd. introduced Japanese rice-paper napkins at its annual holiday dinner party in London. Using paper rather than linen caught on, though many considered it to be something of a social faux pas. That is, until etiquette maven Emily Post wrote, "It's far better form to use paper napkins than linen napkins that were used at breakfast." For an opposing view, Miss Manners retorted in her essential *Guide to Excruciatingly Correct Behavior* that "Saying paper napkins get the job done without having to be laundered is to compare them with paper underwear."

Los Angeles

DRINKING IN HISTORY

It's debatable whether Dorothy Parker once said that Los Angeles is seventy-two suburbs in search of a city. But if she did, no doubt she was inspired by Aldous Huxley who wrote in his 1925 book *Americana* that Los Angeles was nineteen suburbs in search of a metropolis. Either way, the sentiment still resonates.

In old TV shows, whenever characters took a trip to Los Angeles, they'd always have an establishing montage showing the same familiar sites. The Hollywood Sign, Rodeo Drive, La Brea Tar Pits, Olvera Street, and of course, the guy wearing a turban playing guitar on roller skates cruising down the Venice Boardwalk. They never included someone ordering the pickled eggs and a schooner of beer at Joe Jost's. How about a cop eating a machaca burrito at El Tepeyac in Boyle Heights? How about the Sunday brunch crowd enjoying mimosas and lemon/blueberry/ricotta pancakes at the Polo Lounge? What's more L.A. than that?

Maybe Parker was searching for the wrong thing in the wrong place. Perhaps if she'd sat at the bar in Musso & Frank's and ordered a gin martini, she might have seen things differently. Even though Musso &

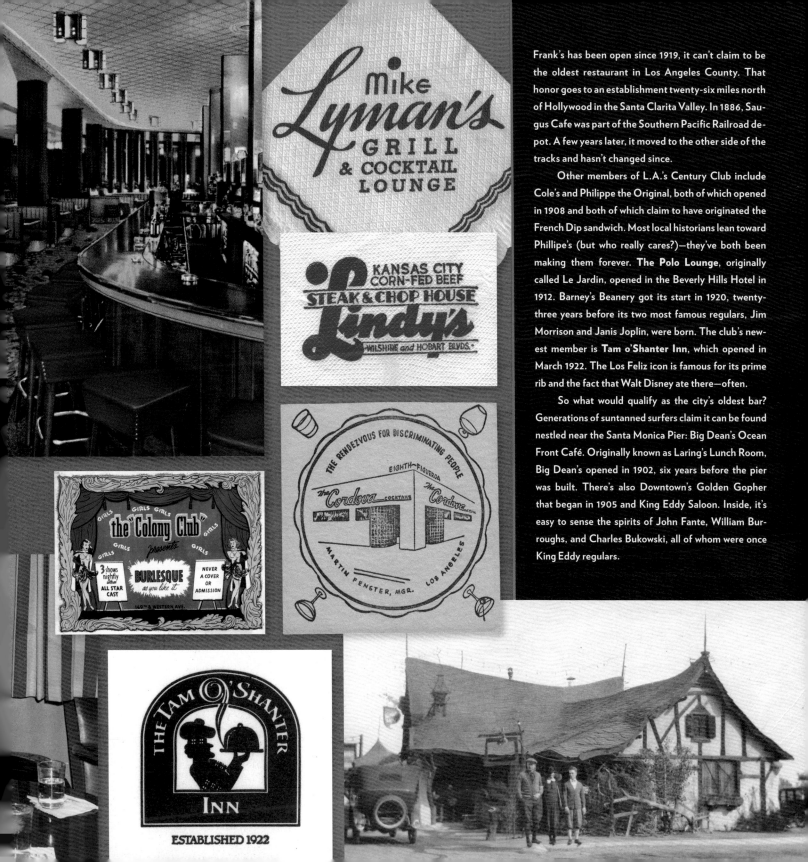

mike Lyman's GRILL & COCKTAIL LOUNGE

KANSAS CITY CORN-FED BEEF
STEAK & CHOP HOUSE
Lindy's
WILSHIRE and HOBART BLVDS.

THE RENDEZVOUS FOR DISCRIMINATING PEOPLE
EIGHTH · FIGUEROA
The Cordova COCKTAILS The Cordova
MARTIN PENSTER, MGR.   LOS ANGELES

the "Colony Club" presents
GIRLS GIRLS GIRLS
GIRLS   GIRLS
3 shows nightly with ALL STAR CAST
BURLESQUE as you like it
NEVER A COVER OR ADMISSION
169th & WESTERN AVE.

The TAM O'SHANTER INN
ESTABLISHED 1922

Frank's has been open since 1919, it can't claim to be the oldest restaurant in Los Angeles County. That honor goes to an establishment twenty-six miles north of Hollywood in the Santa Clarita Valley. In 1886, Saugus Cafe was part of the Southern Pacific Railroad depot. A few years later, it moved to the other side of the tracks and hasn't changed since.

Other members of L.A.'s Century Club include Cole's and Philippe the Original, both of which opened in 1908 and both of which claim to have originated the French Dip sandwich. Most local historians lean toward Phillipe's (but who really cares?)—they've both been making them forever. **The Polo Lounge**, originally called Le Jardin, opened in the Beverly Hills Hotel in 1912. Barney's Beanery got its start in 1920, twenty-three years before its two most famous regulars, Jim Morrison and Janis Joplin, were born. The club's newest member is **Tam o'Shanter Inn**, which opened in March 1922. The Los Feliz icon is famous for its prime rib and the fact that Walt Disney ate there—often.

So what would qualify as the city's oldest bar? Generations of suntanned surfers claim it can be found nestled near the Santa Monica Pier: Big Dean's Ocean Front Café. Originally known as Laring's Lunch Room, Big Dean's opened in 1902, six years before the pier was built. There's also Downtown's Golden Gopher that began in 1905 and King Eddy Saloon. Inside, it's easy to sense the spirits of John Fante, William Burroughs, and Charles Bukowski, all of whom were once King Eddy regulars.

LUCCA

Where dull care is forgotten!

Welcome to Simons

ROBERTS BROS.
SANDWICHES

HOLLYWOOD • LOS ANGELES

Wining & Dining

INTERNATIONAL RESTAURANTS

American restaurants before the turn of the twentieth century were pretty much all about steaks and seafood. But immigrants from Europe slowly began to change the dining landscape. America's oldest Italian restaurant is Fior d'Italia in the North Beach section of San Francisco. Prussian immigrant Henry Schroeder opened Schroeder's Bavarian beer hall in 1893, but it was destroyed in 1906 during the San Francisco Earthquake. It was soon rebuilt, making Schroeder's the oldest German restaurant on the West Coast. But for every ongoing success story, there were hundreds of noteworthy restaurants that are long gone, but still remembered—not just for what they were, but for the resilience of the immigrants who created them.

VINCENT DUNDEE'S

SCOTCH MIST

LA CRESCENTA
CALIFORNIA

the
SHADOWS
RESTAURANT
213 - 2ND AVENUE · SAN MATEO
•
PHONE
DI. 4-5791

Lycoming 7-2426

Viennese

Exotic European Cuisine

Cocktails   Entertainment

544 E. Foothill   San Dimas, California

the Buena Vista

san francisco

Les Freres
TAIX

FRENCH RESTAURANT

In 1906, Umberto (Bert) Rovere arrived at Ellis Island from Turin, Italy. He made his way west and bought a small restaurant in Los Angeles called **Paris Inn Café**. It was such a success that by 1929, Rovere needed a bigger location. At a cost of $300,000, his second incarnation of Paris Inn Café featured a French street scene dominated by a model of the Eiffel Tower. Entertainment included a nine-piece orchestra, singing waiters, and artists dressed in smocks and berets who sketched the patrons. KNX Radio began to broadcast live from the café twice a day. Rovere even composed the music for the "Paris Inn Foxtrot" which became a local hit. Paris Inn Café continued to be popular until 1949, when the entire block was condemned to make way for the new Los Angeles Police Department headquarters. Rovere relocated his Paris Inn Café once again, but this time without the elaborate décor or entertainment. The third incarnation did not last long, and Rovere died seven years after his restaurant closed.

RAVIOLI

Georgio's
ITALIAN VILLAGE
117 N. HILL • OCEANSIDE, CALIF.
Cocktail Lounge

SPAGHETTI

GONDOLA
COCKTAIL *Cafe* LOUNGE

Rudolfo's

4020 EL CA...
REAL
PALO ALTO, CALIF

ITALIAN VILLA
IN OLD SAN GABRIEL
•
Fine Italian Cuisine
GONDOLA
ROOM
COCKTAILS

128 W. MISSION DRIVE
(2 BLOCKS WEST OF THE MISSION)
SAN GABRIEL
PHONE AT-27521

The **ITALIAN
KITCHENS**

COCKTAIL LOUNGE
FRENCH AND
ITALIAN

Marconi
RESTAURANT

Le Lafayette
RESTAURANT
FRANCAIS

*La Villa
Basque*

FRENCH RESTAURANT

GARBINI'S
Real Italian Cuisine
RESTAURANT and COCKTAIL LOUNGE
FINE FOODS *Garbini's Inn* Italian Dinners

3820 Soquel Drive, near 41st Ave.
Between Santa Cruz and Soquel
Phone S.C. G-R.-5-2144

**The Old
VENICE
NOODLE
COMPANY**

2654 MAIN STREET
SANTA MONICA
399-9211

Tokyo Sukiyaki

Fisherman's Wharf
San Francisco, Calif.

Notre Sant...

Ba...
VI...
LOS A...

40

ROSS BROWNING'S

WHITE SANDS

MAGNOLIA CENTER
RIVERSIDE, C...

Morocco Room

2010 EL CAMINO REAL
SAN MATEO, CALIF.

Fireside 5-9683

...soo!

...n
...AGE
...CALIFORNIA

Mardikian's
Omar Khayyam's
Restaurant

Then to the Lip of this poor earthen Urn
I lean'd, the Secret of my Life to learn;
And Lip to Lip it murmur'd — "While you live,
Drink! — for, once dead, you never shall return."

Rubaiyat
COCKTAIL LOUNGE
SAN FRANCISCO

Algiers
RESTAURANT

Resort Motel Redwood City, Califo...

OMAR KHAYYAM'S

GEORGE MARDIKIAN'S
Omar Khayyam's
"FAMOUS ARMENIAN RESTAURANT"
O'FARREL AT POWELL·SAN FRANCISCO·CAL.

Like Umberto Rovere before him, George Magar Mardikian sailed across the Atlantic, entered the U.S. through Ellis Island, and quickly headed west to San Francisco, where he found work as a dishwasher. He had survived the perils, but not the sorrow, of the Armenian Genocide, and said he was proud to now call himself an American.

By 1930, he had moved to California's Central Valley town of Fresno, home to a large Armenian community, where he opened a lunch counter called Omar Khayyam's that was so successful that he was able to open a second restaurant in San Francisco. This second **Omar Khayyam's** was a full-fledged restaurant, with an Arabian Nights theme and an exotic menu filled with Middle Eastern and Armenian fare. It was celebrated as the first restaurant in America to offer Armenian cooking.

In 1944, he published a cookbook, *Dinner at Omar Khayyam's*, and followed that with his memoirs, *Song of America*. In 1951, Mardikian was awarded the Medal of Freedom for his service in the U.S. Army during World War II. He passed away in 1977, and his iconic San Francisco restaurant was destroyed by fire nearly a decade later.

MEXICAN RESTAURANTS

JERRY WILSON'S EL GORDO

JERRY WILSON'S **El Gordo**

8360 E. LAS TUNAS, SAN GABRIEL, CALIF.

WHEN YOU FEEL LIKE A HORSE'S NECK AND NEED A PICK UP REMEMBER **Carls**

LOS ANGELES - PALM SPRINGS

Pierre's R-99 Redlands

The Sweetest Tale South of Heaven

El Coyote MEXICAN FOOD

7312 BEVERLY BOULEVARD
LOS ANGELES, CALIF.
WE 9-2255

Rusty Lantern

9471 MAGNOLIA AVE.
ARLINGTON, CALIF.
MYRT & JAKE

In the heart of Downtown Los Angeles is a touristy-but-historic cobblestone lane called Olvera Street. Tucked amongst the souvenir stands is Cielito Lindo, which has been serving tasty taquitos since 1934. But California's oldest Mexican restaurant is El Cholo on Western Avenue, which opened its doors in 1923. El Coyote opened in 1931 as a tiny café, but moved in 1951 to its present location on Beverly Boulevard. In San Diego, people have been queuing up for the pork tacos at Las Cuatro Milpas since 1933. Travelers taking Route 66 through San Bernardino have been stopping at the Mitla Café since 1937. To the north, in Bakersfield, is Mexicali, where bartenders have been pouring margaritas since 1939.

In many cases the artwork on these vintage napkins celebrates Mexican culture, but some depictions reinforce the negative stereotypes so prevalent in bygone eras. One napkin may show a mariachi serenading a senorita dressed in a traditional Huipil dress. But another might feature a cliched caricature of a sleepy *caballero* taking a siesta under his sombrero. An odd example of this stereotype is found on the napkin for **Pancho's** in Manhattan Beach. Rather than the expected tacos and burritos, the napkin calls out a menu of "Cocktails, Chinese Food, Steaks."

43

CHINESE RESTAURANTS

In 1958, the legendary team of Rodgers & Hammerstein created a new musical on Broadway, *Flower Drum Song*. It was considered a risk at the time since it featured an all-Asian cast. The plot revolved around Sammy Fong, owner of Celestial Garden, a nightclub in San Francisco's Chinatown. The script was based on a book set in a real nightspot, **Forbidden City**.

By the late 1930s, Chinatown was already well-established as a tourist attraction. Most of the big restaurants catered to a largely non-Asian crowd looking for chop suey and chow mein, rather than traditional Cantonese fare. Charlie Low, a gambler who owned **Chinese Village** on Grant Avenue, decided to take his new Forbidden City to the next level. Plush and roomy, the nightclub accommodated a ten-piece orchestra, a troupe of entertainers, and a large dance floor. Every night was a dazzling display: singers, chorus lines, dance teams, and acrobats.

Before long, Forbidden City had competitors. Shanghai Lil, the Lion's Den, Nanking Café, and **Andy Wong's Chinese Sky Room** helped shape the new Chinatown. The Sky Room was well-known for its specialty cocktails including the Dragon's Neck, Dragon's Tail, Dragon's Eye, and of course, the Dragon's Tooth.

44

Suddenly Asian nightclub stars were all the rage, with advertisements comparing them to Caucasian stars. Paul Wing was billed as the "Chinese Fred Astaire"; Larry Ching, the "Chinese Frank Sinatra"; and Toy Yat Mar, the "Chinese Sophie Tucker." Even strippers were compared to others: Noel Toy Young was known as the "Chinese Sally Rand" when she performed her famous bubble dance.

Andy Wong's Chinese Sky Room was famously called "Chinatown's Gayest Nite Club." The nightly dance revue, known as the Wongettes, was featured prominently on its cocktail napkin. But by the early 1960s, the novelty had worn off, and most of these clubs had become discos or topless bars. The Sky Room was the last of the glamorous Chinatown clubs to close its doors.

45

THE CHINA TRADER

Jack Webb is best-known for producing and starring as Sgt. Joe Friday in *Dragnet*, the legendary mid-century cop show that aired both on radio and television. But he was also an avid jazz lover. He owned an extensive record collection and even recorded a handful of albums singing hits like "Try a Little Tenderness" in his own iconic deadpan style. His passion for jazz led him to become a co-owner of **The China Trader**, a tiki bar and restaurant in Burbank. His partner was musician and actor Bobby Troup, who wrote the classic song "Route 66." The two men had something else in common. Webb's first wife was singer Julie London, who married Bobby Troup six years after she and Webb divorced. The three remained friends, and Webb even cast London and Troup in his hit TV show *Emergency*.

The bar was a popular industry hangout, with neighborhood regulars including Lee Marvin and Bob Hope. The cast of the TV show *Hawaiian Eye* came by after shooting wrapped. In 1963, bartender Tony Ramos created a drink to honor the show. Another regular was Gene Roddenberry, who co-wrote episodes of *Dragnet* with Webb before creating the original *Star Trek* series.

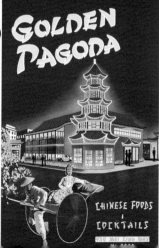

GIN LING WAY
NEW CHINATOWN, LOS ANGELES, CALIFORNIA
© 1952 S. I. CO., L. A.

FORBIDDEN PALACE

COCKTAILS FORBIDDEN PALACE

FORMOSA HOLLYWOOD

On Restaurant Row
BRUCE WONG'S
MING ROOM
358 So. La Cienega Blvd.
Br. 2-6044   Cr. 1-3731

JERRY'S JOYNT
FERGUSON ALLEY
IN OLD CHINATOWN
DANCING   DINING
LOS ANGELES
CALIF.

JERRY'S JOYNT
FERGUSON ALLEY
IN OLD CHINATOWN
LOS ANGELES
CALIF.

TEMPLE OF HEAVEN
Cocktail
Lounge

RICE BOWL
Famous
CHINESE FOODS
NEW
CHINATOWN

MAY ALL WHO ENTER HERE DEPART IN PEACE AND PLENTY
HO TEI
(GOD OF HAPPINESS)
EINAR PETERSEN'S
CHINESE
COCKTAIL
LOUNGE
HOTEL LAFAYETTE   LONG BEACH

CHINESE
JADE LOUNGE
酒家   華玉
454 GIN LING WAY
NEW CHINATOWN
ON BROADWAY

Good Times

BOWLING

The 1950s were the golden age of bowling as both recreation and serious sport. Bowling champions like Dick Anthony and Earl Webber were treated like NBA All-Stars, and tournaments were nationally televised. Leagues started up throughout California. Bowlers could pick up a spare at the **Vallejo Bowl**, roll a strike at the **La Mesa Bowl**, or skip the bowling entirely and just drink at The Gutter.

Highland Park Bowl in northeast Los Angeles is not only the oldest bowling alley in California, but also the tenth oldest alley in the entire country. Built in 1927 during Prohibition, its first tenant was a pharmacy that also operated as a speakeasy offering liquor, live music, as well as a small bowling alley.

In 1966, an Italian immigrant named Joseph Teresa bought the building and opened the lanes to the public, calling it Mr. T's Bowl. By the mid-1980s, the bowl wasn't drawing much of a crowd. New owners started booking punk rock concerts on certain nights, and Mr. T's Bowl became a popular Alternative club.

In 2015, the 1933 Group, which specializes in restoring historic properties, purchased the building, uncovered the original décor, including the bowling alley's eight wooden lanes, and re-established its original name, Highland Park Bowl.

Haps
milt and Julie
PLEASANTON, CALIFORNIA

Turf Club
HOME OF FINE FOODS

9001 ANAHEIM-TELEGRAPH ROAD • RIVERA, CALIFORNIA

$10
Santa
Handica

AZUCAR
  GEO. WOOLF – '3
TOP ROW
  W.D. WRIGHT – '3
ROSEMONT
  H. RICHARDS – '3
STAGEHAND
  N. WALL – '3
KAYAK II
  J. ADAMS – '3
SEA BISCUIT
  J. POLLARD – '4
BAY VIEW
  N. WALL –
THUMBS UP
  J. LONGDEN – '
WAR KNIGHT
  J. ADAMS – '
OLHAVERRY
  M. PETERSON
TALON
  E. ARCA'
VULCAN FOR
  D. G

Smith's
Coral Room

721 WEST HUNTINGTON DRIVE
ARCADIA

Jimmy
Diamond's

5th at E, San Bernardino, Calif.

Sam Meye

ALL I SAID
LET ME HAVE T
THE NOSE – AN

50

HORSE RACING

The Derby opened in 1931 in Arcadia, three years before the world-famous Santa Anita Racetrack ran its first race on Christmas Day, 1934. It was another four years before the two places were forever connected.

George Woolf, nicknamed "The Iceman," was one of the greatest jockeys of his day. His career highlight was riding Seabiscuit to victory in the 1938 Triple Crown race, an event immortalized in the 2003 film *Seabiscuit*. Later that same year, he and a partner bought the Derby. It soon became the first and last stop for anyone who was serious about a day at the races. Whether it was breakfast while perusing the *Racing News*, or dinner and drinks to celebrate how well those bets paid off.

Woolf was killed when his horse threw him during a race in 1946. His widow ran the Derby for five more years before selling it to Dominic and Lorene Sturniolo, who went on to manage the place for nearly sixty years. It was sold again in 2007, but it is rich with horse-racing memorabilia including tributes to George Woolf.

TURF CLUB

NO PLACE OR SHOW—
ALWAYS A WINNER HERE!
· FOR ·
GOOD FOOD, DRINKS, COCKTAILS AND ENVIRONMENT

ANAHEIM TELEGRAPH ROAD AT ROSEMEAD RIVER

Founded by Jockey George Woolf–1938

The DERBY

Arcadia, Calif.

PORPOISE ROOM

Marineland of the Pacific opened in 1954, a year before Disneyland. It was not only one of California's first theme parks, at the time it was the world's largest marine oceanarium. Along with dolphins, sea lions, harbor seals, and sharks, Marineland was home to a pair of beloved orcas named Orky and Corky, who starred in their own show. In the **Porpoise Room**, diners enjoyed an ocean view while sipping a King Neptune cocktail served in a coconut shell. Hollywood took advantage of the underwater setting to shoot the TV series *Sea Hunt* with Lloyd Bridges and Roger Corman's cult classic movie *Attack of the Crab Monsters*.

By the mid-1980s, Marineland was run down and barely breaking even. Its main competitor, Sea World in San Diego, took it over, closed the park, and trucked Orky and Corky to Sea World. Marineland sat abandoned until 2007 when it was finally bulldozed to make way for a private resort.

THE LITTLE SHRIMP

Laguna Beach has long been a gay oasis, and its voters elected Bob Gentry, one of the country's first openly gay candidates, as mayor and city councilman from 1982 to 1996. In 1995, word got out that the Laguna Beach gay bar **The Little Shrimp** would be closing—after thirty years in operation—because of a dispute over property repairs.

The Shrimp, as the regulars called it, was in many ways, a relic from a different era. Unlike its rowdier neighbors, the Fleur de Lys and the Boom-Boom Room, the Shrimp was an old-school piano bar where Broadway show tunes ruled the night. The main entertainer was Rudy de la Mor, known for his outrageous hats and bawdy sense of humor. For decades, the Shrimp was an integral part of the town's gay social scene, alongside beachfront bars like Dante and Barefoot.

But the closing of the Little Shrimp was a sign of the times. By the mid-1990s, the city once known as "San Francisco South," had become gentrified by high rents and increasing conservatism.

the
Little
Shrimp
1305 S. COAST HIGHWAY
LAGUNA BEACH
PH. 494-4111

EL RANCHO
MOTEL & RESTAURANT
COCKTAILS
MERMAID
Room
MILLBRAE, CALIFORNIA

Beverly Wilshire

Bimbo's 365 Club
"HOME OF THE GIRL IN THE FISH BOWL"

Mermaids

SWIMMING NIGHTLY AT A BAR NEAR YOU

In the 1950s and '60s, porthole lounges were popular across the country. Large windows behind the bar provided views into aquariums and swimming pools. Women dressed as mermaids would cavort among the underwater fauna. The original idea dates back to Billy Rose's Aquacade at the 1939 New York World's Fair. It wasn't long before the concept reached California. Both the El Rancho Motel in Millbrae and the Hacienda Hotel in Fresno had a **Mermaid Room**, but the **Reef Lounge** in San Diego's Stardust Motor Hotel offered an unusual twist. There were four shows per night, but the last one at 11 o'clock was adults-only, since the mermaids discarded their seashells and swam topless.

ROBERTS FISH GROTTO and GRILL
1211 Kay Street
Sacramento
Calif.

Alioto's
NO. 8
Recommended by Duncan Hines in his book "Adventures in Good Eating"

DINE AT THE SIGN OF THE SWORDFISH

Sam's Sea Food Spa
2501 COAST HIGHWAY
SEAL BEACH

Stardust
MOTOR HOTEL
IN MISSION VALLEY · SAN DIEGO

* 27 HOLE GOLF COURSE
* 18 HOLE PITCH AND PUTT COURSE
* 2 HEATED POOLS

Coral Room
DINING AND DANCING
EVERY NIGHT

Crane Room
* FOR SUPERB DINING
* BANQUET AND CONFERENCE FACILITIES

Reef Lounge
VISION LEVEL POOL
WITH PICTURE WINDOW

UNDERWATER BALLET
8 P.M. 9 P.M. 10 P.M. 11 P.M.
EVERY NIGHT

Vista Del Mar
RESTAURANT
FISHERMAN'S WHARF
SAN FRANCISCO

Mels

DRIVE IN RESTAURANTS IN NORTHERN CALIFORNIA

1 SAN FRANCISCO
MISSION NEAR GENEVA AVE.

2 SAN FRANCISCO
GEARY AND BEAUMONT

3 SAN FRANCISCO
SOUTH VAN NESS NEAR
MISSION

4 SAN JOSE
SANTA CLARA AT 16TH

5 SALINAS
909 SO. MAIN

6 BERKELEY
SHATTUCK AND
CHANNING WAY

7 OAKLAND
17TH AND SAN PABLO

8 WALNUT CREEK
WALNUT CREEK

9 SACRAMENTO
SACRAMENTO

A History of Cocktail Napkins

In 1886, a news feature ran in the *Kansas City Farmer* with the headline "Japanese Napkins: Funny Little Mouth-Wipers Made From Rice Paper." The article notes that paper napkins had become all the rage with housewives, hotels, and in boarding houses. After the writer visited a local Japanese gift shop, he described them as "bordered with pale blue Mandarins, each one trying to hit his neighbor with a mushroom-shaped parasol, while a big Mandarin sat in the center in seeming bliss." Even in the 1800s, cocktail napkins with cute cartoons were a popular item.

San Francisco

In 1906, devastated by an estimated 7.9 earthquake and resultant fires, nearly three-quarters of the city of San Francisco was in ruins. But a handful of bars and restaurants not only survived the catastrophe, they continue to thrive more than two centuries later: Tadich Grill in the financial district, the Old Ship Saloon at the Embarcadero, Shotwell's in the Mission District, and Fior d'Italia in North Beach, the oldest Italian restaurant in the United States.

BREEN'S CAFE & TOMMY'S JOYNT

Since the mid-1860s, there have been two major newspapers in San Francisco, the *Chronicle* and the *Examiner*. Each paper's staff had a favorite watering hole. For years, journalists from the *Chronicle* hung out at M & M Tavern. Reporters from the *Examiner* gathered at **Breen's Cafe**, which claimed to have the longest bar in the city. At noon, the bartenders lined up shot glasses along the counter in anticipation of the lunch crowd. Both places were more than just drinking establishments. They were hofbraus, a type of bar that offered cheap meals to their drinking patrons. The choices were simple: corned beef, roast chicken, or ribs served with sides of canned vegetables and rolls. Other popular hofbraus included Brennan's, the Starlite, and **Tommy's Joynt** which opened in 1947. These were the kinds of places where men started their day with boilermakers for breakfast, and at mid-day, lunch included a couple of old-fashioneds. Both Breen's and the M & M Tavern closed in the late 1980s, but well into the twenty-first century, Tommy's Joynt is still serving its famous turkey dinners, still complete with two sides and a roll.

DIMING · DANCING
at
Joe DiMaggio's
FISHERMANS WHARF
IN SAN FRANCISCO·
VISIT OUR LOUNGE
FEATURING
Joe DiMaggio
COCKTAIL

SAN FRANCISCO'S
MOST BEAUTIFUL
COCKTAIL LOUNGE
STARLIGHT
ROOM
"AN INN OF QUALITY"
1121 MARKET ST.

TINY'S
437-439 Powell St.
San Francisco

YOU ARE A STRANGER HERE BUT ONCE
BLUE
GOLD
136 TURK ST.
San Francisco, Calif
ORdway 2040

A HIT!
LEFTY
O'DOUL'S
Cocktail BAR
209 POWELL ST.
SAN FRANCISCO
N · E
USE THE COMPASS TO FIND YOUR WAY BACK

LEFTY O'DOUL'S & JOE DIMAGGIO'S

Joe DiMaggio and Lefty O'Doul were both born in San Francisco, and both played in the minor leagues for the San Francisco Seals. Both went on to become New York Yankees, though not at the same time. O'Doul was a relief pitcher for just a few seasons while DiMaggio was a three-time MVP for the Yanks. The two men had one other thing in common, they both had restaurants in San Francisco.

After DiMaggio's first year with the Yankees, he opened **Joe DiMaggio's Grotto**, a seafood restaurant on Fisherman's Wharf. In 1954, after Joe married Marilyn Monroe, the couple moved into a house not far from the Grotto, but their union ended in less than a year. DiMaggio eventually sold his interest in the restaurant, but its legend lives on.

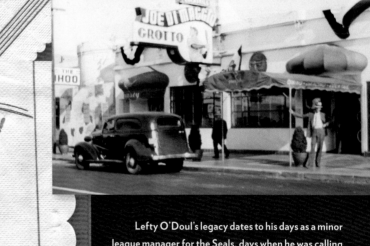

Lefty O'Doul's legacy dates to his days as a minor league manager for the Seals, days when he was calling the shots for a young DiMaggio. After O'Doul finally retired from baseball, he opened **Lefty O'Doul's**, a hofbrau in Union Square. Its new owner Nick Bovis lost his lease in 2017 and tried reopening the place at Fisherman's Wharf, not far from where DiMaggio's had been. But after an FBI probe of public corruption, the restaurant closed its doors.

THE COMMUTER LOUNGE
500 MISSION ST.   SAN FRANCISCO

THE TAP ROOM LOUNGE
BAY BRIDGE TERMINAL · LOWER FLOOR · SAN FRANCISCO

the Lighthouse Lounge
A. SABELLA'S
SEA FOOD GROTTO

2770 TAYLOR   SAN FRANCISCO, CALIF.
AT FISHERMAN'S WHARF

YOUR HOST
George Kammerer
techau
247 POWELL ST., San Francisco

techau
COCKTAILS
247 POWELL ST.

Friday
after
Thanksgiving
Day, 11/28/47.
with
Mom &
Aunt Frances
San Francisco

60

DOMINO CLUB

Tucked away in a small alley off the financial district, **Domino Club** was a high-end nightclub that featured popular jazz bands. Owner Charlie Anderson, an art collector, displayed his collection of old-world nude paintings on its walls. On certain nights, Italian artist Roberto Lupetti painted portraits of nude models while diners watched. Years later, the Vatican hired Lupetti to help restore the Sistine Chapel. Another Domino artist, Irving Sinclair, painted a large nude called *Gloria*, which hung over the main bar. Ads for the club invited patrons to "Meet Gloria at the Domino Club."

DESERT OUTPOST

BEAUMONT
CALIFORNIA

Newman's
EL ENCANTO

AZUSA, CALIF.

EDGEWOOD
4-9050

OPEN 24 HOURS DAILY

Farnesi's
FINE FOOD
LIQUORS

COCKTAILS

...ING and DANCING
...OCKTAIL LOUNGE

500 Hi-way 99 Chowchilla

Dining
Dancing

Costella's Chalet

Felton, California
Phone Felton 5-9977

Bus & Bob's

TOWN HALL
COCKTAILS
CAFE

COMPLETE DINNER
DANCING
CRESTLINE
PHONE - 6554

GARDEN RENDEZVOUS CAFE

VISIT OUR COCKTAIL ROOM
Pasadena

3035 HUNTINGTON DRIVE

JUST EAST OF SAN GABRIEL BLVD.

Arches Cafe

and COCKTAIL LOUNGE
NEWPORT-BALBOA

Since 1849

Sycamore
INN

BEAR GULCH
CUCAMONGA, CALIF.
HIGHWAY 66

's Tavern

Gori Tavern

THE RUSSIAN RIVER
ville, California

"OUR PATRONS ARE THE BEST PEOPLE IN THE WORLD"

Normandy

The
Normandy
OCEANSIDE,
CALIFORNIA

The Farmhouse

YORKSHIRE 7-5628
ON EL CAMINO REAL BETWEEN
MOUNTAIN VIEW AND PALO ALTO
AT LOS ALTOS

Architecture

SYCAMORE INN

In the mid 1800s, William Rubottom—"Uncle Billy" to those who knew him—had come west from Missouri. He opened Uncle Billy's Rubottom Tavern Inn on the road between San Bernardino and Los Angeles. The Inn was famed for its Southern cooking and Uncle Billy's eccentric behavior. Legend goes that three slave-owners from Missouri accusing him of either emancipating or borrowing some of their slaves, depending on which version one hears. Either way, Uncle Billy was shot but still managed to kill all three men with a knife. He also shot his son-in-law Horace Bell, an ugly drunk who abused Billy's daughter. When she'd had enough and came to her father for protection, Bell showed up demanding that Billy hand her over. Apparently, Uncle Billy was quicker on the draw than Horace.

According to another local legend, Billy also brought a pair of possums with him from Missouri. The plan was to breed enough to put them on the Inn's menu as a Southern delicacy. The locals weren't interested, so he released the critters, offspring of whom soon began to spread across the state, officially introducing possums to California.

William Rubottom passed away in 1885, and in 1920, local rancher John Klusman began construction on the building that still stands today. Then in 1939, Danish immigrant Irl Hinrichsen bought the Inn and changed its name to **Sycamore Inn**. New owners took over in 2002, but possum was never on the menu.

Andary's
SUPPER CLUB • DRIVE-IN
5920 SOUTH ATLANTIC BLVD.
LU. 8607
LO. 5-4334

39 CEDARWAY
ENTRANCE TO
THE PIKE

BALLYHOO
PAY TWISS
LOUNGE

LONG BEACH,
CALIF.
PHONE
606-18

PLAZA COCKTAILS
P

406 BASELINE
San Bernardino,
CALIF.

COCKTAILS
FINER FOODS
PARTIES • SOCIALS • BANQUETS

Linko's
Linko's

188 EAST I STREET • COLTON, CALIF.
PHONES 2631-2552

• FREE PARKING •

STEAKS
CHICKEN
INDIGO
Cocktails
AIR
CONDITIONED

SID AND CLODIE BROWN'S
Cafe INDIGO
4-269 LANKERSHIM BLVD.
NORTH HOLLYWOOD
SUNSET 2-9375
"Intimate
Entertainment
Nightly"

Ferguson's
FINE FOODS

Ferguson's

FOR FINER DRINKS, COCKTAILS
AND TASTY DELICIOUS FOODS
IT'S ALWAYS —

Ferguson's
THOMPSON BLVD. AT ARCADE
VENTURA

Vi
DINI
South

**SPORTSMANS
TAVERN**
SERVING WILD GAME & TROUT
ALSO CHICKEN & STEAKS
LUNCHEONS 11:30 to 2 TUESDAY thru SATURDAY
COCKTAILS

PHONE ELLIOTT 8-2186
1452 EAST HUNTINGTON DRIVE
DUARTE, CALIF.
[CLOSED MONDAYS]

GARDEN OF ALLAH

Vivian Connor was barely out of high school when she married and—just as quickly—filed for divorce, leaving Vivian Laird with a new name and a settlement of $2,500, money she used to open her **Garden of Allah** in Long Beach. When Prohibition ended in 1933, Garden of Allah had the first liquor license in Long Beach. Business was so good that Laird sold the first restaurant and opened a larger Garden of Allah in Seal Beach, which featured live music and a dance floor. She then went on to open **Bohemia**, a lounge in Long Beach's Robinson Hotel, **Brass Rail Café** in Laguna Beach, and the South Seas in Anaheim. In 1947, she opened **Vivian Laird's**, a high-end supper club in Long Beach that featured its Jungle Room bar.

Robert Holstun bought Laird's Garden of Allah, but the Long Beach bunco squad busted him in 1957 for running a "B" girl drunk-roll racket at one of his other bars, the Gyro Room. Holstun was forced to sell Garden of Allah to Reverend Guy Newton who planned to convert the nightclub into a Baptist church. Rev. Newton's plans fell through, but it did go on to become Larry Goldfinger's Go-Go, a topless club. The last incarnation, Surfer Girl A-Go-Go, was finally bulldozed and replaced with a Jack-In-the-Box.

Cute Critters

SCOTTIES, KITTENS, ZEBRAS, ROOSTERS & MORE

Advertising and animals go hand in hand, or at least hand in paw. Even when it comes to promoting alcohol. In the 1890s, James Buchanan conceived of a blended Scotch whiskey he originally called "House of Commons" after the British House of Commons. But due to its two-tone label, most customers simply referred to it as "Black & White" whiskey. Buchanan had a pair of dogs, a black Scottish Terrier and a West Highland White Terrier. He decided to put them on the label and ever since, Scotties have been associated with scotch.

In 1929, Guinness Beer began an advertising campaign featuring animals enjoying a pint along with the slogan "My Goodness, My Guinness." Artist John Gilroy's posters featured everything from sea lions to penguins, a kangaroo, and most famously a toucan. Across the pond in Minnesota, Hamm's developed its own cute animal mascot, the Hamm's Beer Bear. In the 1950s, he was featured in a series of animated TV commercials that were so popular, the Minneapolis newspapers listed them in the daily broadcast schedule. Budweiser has been using animals as their "spokesperson" for years: the Clydesdale Horses, the infamous Spuds MacKenzie, not to mention a variety of talking frogs, gecko lizards, and the occasional cute puppy.

These days, society tends to frown on the notion of a cuddly bear kicking back with a cold, frosty one. We'd prefer to drink a Dos Equis with the Most Interesting Man in the World than a Bud Light with a bull terrier.

The Zebra Room
THE TOWN HOUSE
LOS ANGELES

Zebra Room
The Town House · Los Angeles

ROBERTS-AT-THE-BEACH

Roberts'
AT THE
BEACH

ON THE WAY TO ROBERTS' IN
THE GAY 90'S
SINCE
1897

After running a chicken farm for thirty years, Dominic Roberts decided to buy a roadhouse near the San Francisco Bay called the Sea Breeze and renamed it **Roberts-at-the-Beach**. After Dominic passed away, his oldest son "Shorty" Roberts took over. A racetrack regular, Shorty decorated the bar with paintings of thoroughbreds, staged rocking-horse races on the dance floor, and even made a bet with the manager of Bay Meadows Racetrack that his horse Blackie could swim from the bar to the Golden Gate Bridge. Blackie made the crossing in twenty-three minutes, with Shorty swimming behind him, one hand clutching the horse's tail.

"BLACKIE"
SWIMMING THE GOLDEN GATE
SAN FRANCISCO, CALIF.

CALIFORNIA HOTEL
COCKTAIL LOUNGE
SAN BERNARDINO, CALIF.

Clearman's
Golden Cock Inn
for
chicken
Rosemead & Huntington Drive

George Jr. Club Cafe Cocktails
Cocktails
364-372 Highland Ave.
San Bernardino,
California
Phone
89-131
89-193

COCKTAIL TIME

COCKTAIL TIME

THE RICKY SHAY ROOM

220 W. Valley Blvd., Alhambra

IN
FONTANA
IT'S
Harold's
FOR
Cocktails
AND
Charcoal Broiled
Steaks & Chops
For Reservations Phone 6704

Steve's
RED ROOSTER
CAFE & COCKTAIL LOUNGE
VICTORVILLE, CALIF.

HOTEL Statler

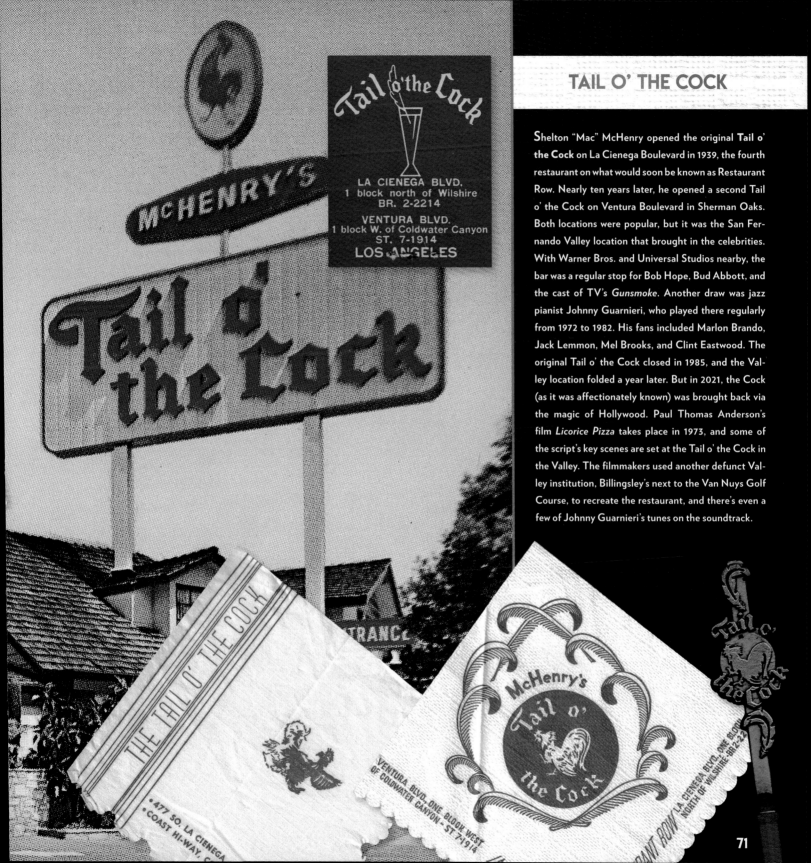

TAIL O' THE COCK

Shelton "Mac" McHenry opened the original **Tail o' the Cock** on La Cienega Boulevard in 1939, the fourth restaurant on what would soon be known as Restaurant Row. Nearly ten years later, he opened a second Tail o' the Cock on Ventura Boulevard in Sherman Oaks. Both locations were popular, but it was the San Fernando Valley location that brought in the celebrities. With Warner Bros. and Universal Studios nearby, the bar was a regular stop for Bob Hope, Bud Abbott, and the cast of TV's *Gunsmoke*. Another draw was jazz pianist Johnny Guarnieri, who played there regularly from 1972 to 1982. His fans included Marlon Brando, Jack Lemmon, Mel Brooks, and Clint Eastwood. The original Tail o' the Cock closed in 1985, and the Valley location folded a year later. But in 2021, the Cock (as it was affectionately known) was brought back via the magic of Hollywood. Paul Thomas Anderson's film *Licorice Pizza* takes place in 1973, and some of the script's key scenes are set at the Tail o' the Cock in the Valley. The filmmakers used another defunct Valley institution, Billingsley's next to the Van Nuys Golf Course, to recreate the restaurant, and there's even a few of Johnny Guarnieri's tunes on the soundtrack.

I'M IN THE DOG HOUSE!

El Curtola
RESTAURANT

510 17th Street

OAKLAND, CALIFORNIA

THE DRINKS ARE ON ME

YOU NAME IT—
I'LL DRINK IT!

I'D SWEAR I'M
SEEIN' PEOPLE

Pink Elephants

THE ULTIMATE NAPKIN CRITTER

In the early 1800s, Americans drank more alcohol than any other time in the country's history. Those were the days of cheap corn whiskey, so people tended to get a little sloppy on Saturday night, often to the point of drunken hallucinations, which back then, were called "seeing snakes in your boots."

Those snakes may have been more than just a colorful turn of phrase. In the early 1900s, a London physician who studied alcoholics suffering from *delirium tremens* found that his patients' eyeballs were congested, and the movement of retinal blood vessels resembled the squirming of black snakes. Along with snakes, they imagined red rats, blue monkeys, and the occasional green giraffe. But if we stretch our imaginations, P.T. Barnum could be given credit for making pink elephants the preferred term for inebriation. He and his partner James Bailey operated the Barnum & Bailey Circus. In 1884, the circus's big act was going to be the first white elephant in the U.S. It turned out to be a gray elephant with a pink patch across its face. The ensuing bad publicity probably drove P.T. to drink.

In 1932, Guy Lombardo had a hit with the song "Pink Elephants." But it was Walt Disney who made pink elephants the official symbol of going on a bender. Disney's 1941 animated feature *Dumbo* has a dream sequence brought on when Dumbo and his pal, Timothy Q. Mouse, accidently drink Champagne. It's a kaleidoscope of pink elephants singing, dancing, and morphing into wondrous psychedelic imagery.

VERMOUTH COCKTAIL

1 dash bitters
1 dash Maraschino
1 wineglass Vermouth

Fill glass with ice. Frappe. Strain and serve with cherry.
May use ½ Italian and ½ French Vermouth if desired.

MAIDEN'S PRAYER COCKTAIL

¾ oz. dry Gin
¾ oz. Cointreau
¼ oz. orange juice
¼ oz. lemon juice

Stir with cracked ice. Strain into large chilled cocktail glass.

CUBA LIBRE

1½ oz. Jamaica Rum
Juice of ½ lime

Put lime juice in glass. Drop in lime shell. Add ice cubes
and Rum. Fill glass with cola and serve.

SKOAL!

PROST

CHEERIO

BOTTOMS UP

SALUTE

SIDECAR

Gipper

THE COCKAIL CROWD

A History of Cocktail Napkins

The Scott Paper Company was founded in 1879 and grew to become the biggest manufacturer of paper sanitary products in the world. In 1890, it was the first company to put toilet paper on a roll, and in 1913, it introduced paper tissues. But it was in 1957 that Scott started marketing pastel-colored paper napkins to the general public, a full seventy years after John Dickinson Ltd. brought the first paper napkins to London from Japan.

The THISTLE INN

2395 GLENDALE BLVD.
LOS ANGELES 46, CALIF.

NO 3-8243

DUKE'S
119 WEST 1 ST,
COLTON
WEST   1 ST.

CLOVER CLUB
1276 E. BASE LINE
BASE   LINE
SAN BERNARDINO

123 CLUB
123 NO. MT. VERNON
RIALTO   AVE.

tid-two cocktail lounge

6573 SHATTUCK
OAKLAND, CALIF.

dinner with albert
Sat. P.M. 10/18/52.

Sea Wolf RESTAURANT

Foot of Broadway • Oakland, California

BOMBO

TEL.
TE. 2-6551

Oscar's of Oakland

550 GREEN ST.
SAN FRANCISCO
CALIF.

CAPRI
COCKTAIL LOUNGE

510 17TH STREET
OAKLAND
CALIF.

Christmas Eve
after work
12/24/42
Campbell Tom &
Yvonne

Clark's
404 Fourteenth St.
Oakland, Calif.

topp's
Cocktails

Corner 105th Ave. & E. 14th St.
Oakland, Calif.

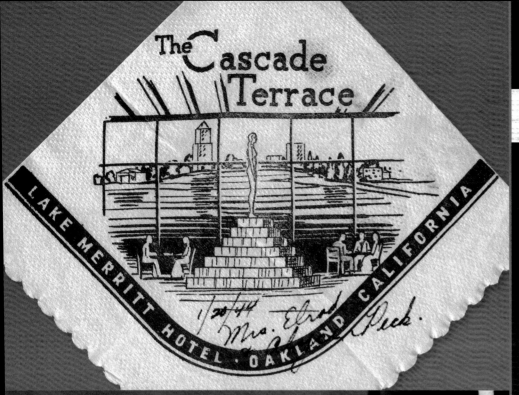

The Cascade Terrace
LAKE MERRITT HOTEL · OAKLAND CALIFORNIA

Oscar's of Oakland

Oscar's
3285 LAKESHORE
Oakland, California

SHOWBOAT

Jack London Square is one of the oldest neighborhoods in Oakland. It's where author Jack London grew up and later spent time at the First and Last Chance Saloon writing his novels, *Call of the Wild* (1903) and *The Sea-Wolf* (1904). Officially declared Jack London Square in 1951, the area became a nightlife destination, with **Showboat**, a floating restaurant built on a converted riverboat, as its main attraction. Along with drinks and dining, Showboat had live music and a dance floor. But in the autumn of 1956, a fire broke out below deck, and the ship sank to the bottom of the harbor.

Showboat is long gone, but the First and Last Chance Saloon lives on. In fact, it's one of the oldest bars in California, having opened its doors in 1848. The name comes from a time when the bar was a sailor's first and last chance to have a drink before or after shipping out. It's still, as original owner Johnny Heinold once said, a saloon where seafaring and waterfront men can feel at ease.

SHOWBOAT
RESTAURANT

Steak & B.B.Q.

POOR RED'S BAR-B-Q

Poor Red's Bar-B-Q was originally built as a Wells Fargo stagecoach stop in a little town called El Dorado, just a bit east of Sacramento. that brought in supplies for gold miners. Once the Gold Rush peaked, it served as a doctor's office and a grocery store. Then in the late 1920s, it became a saloon known as Kelly's Bar. Business picked up when Highway 49 was built, so Kelly partnered with a man called Poor Red to sell barbecue in the bar. But the friendship soured, so they had a dice game to decide who would buy the other out. Kelly lost, and the bar became Poor Red's Bar-B-Q.

For decades, the restaurant was popular mostly with locals. Then in 1952, a newly engaged couple asked bartender Frank Klein to create a special cocktail that would match their brand-new gold Cadillac. After a few misfires, Klein came up with what he called the Golden Cadillac. A combination of Bols White Crème de Cacao, Galliano L'Autentico, half and half, and ice all combined in a blender. He served it in a champagne glass and poured the rest in a sidecar, which is how it's still served today. Word spread and tourists from across the state were stopping in to try the bar's signature drink. In 1999, the Galliano Company proclaimed Poor Red's Bar-B-Q as the largest Galliano consumer in the world.

Red and his wife Opal both passed away, and the restaurant's new owners let it fall into disrepair. In 2013, they were arrested for tax evasion and insurance fraud. The restaurant sat empty and abandoned for three years. Then new owners took over and brought it back to its former glory. If you're ever on Highway 49, stop on by and try a couple of Golden Cadillacs.

SADDLE AND SIRLOIN

Arthur and David Lyons launched the **Saddle and Sirloin** restaurant in Studio City in 1947. An old-school steakhouse, it featured red leather booths and decidedly western décor. The brothers went on to open three more branches in Glendale, Bakersfield, and Palm Springs, each with a bar and a stage featuring comedians and live music. One regular performer was piano man Matt Dennis who played with Dick Haymes and Tommy Dorsey. Mae West was a fan, who always showed up when Dennis was at the keyboard. Another group who played the Saddle and Sirloin were the 4 Jokers. Mixing music and comedy, their act included improvised skits, celebrity impressions, and instrumental dance tunes. The highlight each evening was something they called the "Lucky Lasagna Hit Parade." Mae West ended up buying the Studio City restaurant, which she renamed the Showcase.

In 1964, Showcase became a nightclub called Queen Mary Show Lounge, with a cabaret featuring female impersonators, drag comics, and male strippers. The Queen Mary closed in 2003, replaced by Serra's Dine and Dance, a Turkish supper club. What would Mae West think of all this?

EATON'S

Paul Cummins opened a chain of upscale steak houses called **Eaton's**. All five locations were popular, especially the Rancho in Studio City, near Republic Film Studios. Its menu offered a Gene Autry Sandwich honoring the studio's singing cowboy star. But Cummins's restaurant career had started in the 1950s, when he opened Huddle, and Googie diners were all the rage, thanks to the David Bowie of architecture, John Lautner. He inspired a wave of diners, motels, and gas stations that looked straight out of an episode of *The Jetsons*. A major part of the Mid-Century Modern aesthetic, Googie was equally influenced by Cadillac fins, flying saucers, and the crazy music of Esquivel, the King of Space-Age Pop. Cummins hired Armet & Davis, the architects who cornered the Googie market. Popular chains such as Denny's, Sambo's, and Bob's Big Boy were Armet & Davis designs. Two of their coffee shops—Norms and Pann's—are icons of the genre. The first restaurant Armet & Davis designed for Cummins was Huddle, also on La Cienega, which was followed by a second located near the Santa Monica Airport. The Santa Monica Huddle offered six dining options including the Sky Room cocktail lounge and the Scottish-themed Heather Room.

Clearman's
Steak'n Stein Inn

for CHARCOAL
BROILED
STEAKS
9545 WHITTIER BLVD.
PICO, CALIFORNIA

Clearman's
STEAK'n STEIN
INN

Bashful Bull
Candlelight Dining
29827 Mission Blvd.   Hayward, Calif.
at
Holiday Bowl
Always Open
JE 8-0300

The
HICKORY
HB
BARBECUE
Corona, California

83

Monticello Cafe

1222 W. 7th STREET
LOS ANGELES

DINE AND

DANCE

Music & Dancing

LOST WEEKEND & HOUSE OF HARMONY

Lost Weekend and House of Harmony not only had the same owner, but both featured live keyboard music. Beyond that, they were quite different. The House of Harmony was a gay piano bar on Polk Street in San Francisco. Polk Gulch was the city's main LGBTQ neighborhood from the 1950s until the early 1980s. But rising rents and the influx of curious tourists drove most of the city's gay population to the Castro District.

Lost Weekend was in North Beach and the main attraction was a large Wurlitzer organ. Named after the classic 1945 film, *The Lost Weekend*, which starred Ray Milland as an alcoholic trying to get sober. There's a painting of Al, who ran the place, serving a drink to a desperate-looking Milland. For years the house organist was Larry Vannucci, who had been classically trained, but played all the old standards. Occasionally "One-Arm Alice," a regular, would accompany him with her left-hand. In the late '60s, Vannucci got another gig and Al brought in a new organ player, Anton LaVey, who went on to form the Church of Satan.

LOST WEEKEND
1940 TARAVAL STREET
COCKTAILS
HOUSE OF HARMONY
1312 POLK STREET

JIMMY DIAMOND'S
Uptowner
REGGIE SAVIO and JIMMY DIAMOND

WILL KING'S
Koffee Kup
and
RUMPUS ROOM
with
HERMIE KING
AT THE PIANO
GEARY BLVD. AT 18th AVE.
SAN FRANCISCO
CALIFORNIA

"rug cutters"

JAZZ WORKSHOP

In the mid-1950s, the North Beach section of San Francisco was Ground Zero for the Beat Generation. It was also the epicenter of the city's jazz scene. On a Saturday night, you could club-hop down Broadway and catch sets by Stan Getz at the **Jazz Workshop**, Duke Ellington at Basin Street West, T-Bone Walker at the Sugar Hill, and the Modern Jazz Quartet at El Matador. But it was at the Jazz Workshop that most of the neighborhood's artists and writers congregated. One night in 1961, comedian Lenny Bruce was on the bill along with saxophonist Ben Webster. After Bruce did his 10 pm set, he was arrested for indecency, and taken directly to night court, where the first judge was inclined to lock him up. But Bruce's lawyer managed to get him before a second judge who was more sympathetic. This was the same magistrate who just four years earlier had acquitted City Lights publisher Lawrence Ferlinghetti of obscenity charges for publishing Allen Ginsberg's revolutionary poem "Howl." The comedian put up his bail and was able to get back to the Jazz Workshop in time to do his 1 am set. The North Beach jazz scene lasted thirty years before business slowed and one by one, the clubs closed including the Jazz Workshop which had its last show in 1983.

Lydia & Leonard's
GUYS & DOLLS

Cocktails and Piano Bar Entertainment

3755 E. COLORADO ST. PASADENA, CALIF.

Ti-Tones
Continuous Entertainment

4 P.M. – 2 A.M.

711 EL CAMINO REAL

REDWOOD CITY

CALIFORNIA

VIENI VIENI

Operatic Entertainment

World's Best Cappuccino

1313 Stockton St.   EX. 2-9910
SAN FRANCISCO

JAZZ WORKSHOP

**473 BROADWAY
SAN FRANCISCO, CALIF.**

87

Souvenir Photo
OF A MARVELOUS EVENING

AMERICA'S FINEST ORCHESTRAS
WORLD FAMOUS
HOLLYWOOD
★ Palladium

SOUVENIR PHOTO

Hollywood PALLADIUM Dancing Nightly

Hollywood Palladium Caterers

HOLLYWOOD
CALIFORNIA

Souvenir Photo of A Wonderful Evening
with
LAWRENCE WELK
AND HIS CHAMPAGNE MUSIC

THE ALL-NEW WORLD FAMOUS
Hollywood PALLADIUM

SOUVENIR PH...

"Where The Important Events Happen"

World-Famous HOLLYWOOD
PALLADIUM
HOLLYWOOD, CALIFORNIA

World-Famous HOLLYWOOD
PALLADIUM
HOLLYWOOD, CALIFORNIA

HOLLYWOOD

Palladium

World Famous Home of America's
Greatest Dance Orchestras

Sunset near Vine Street ~ Hollywood, California

HOLLYWOOD PALLADIUM

The **Hollywood Palladium** opened on New Year's Eve, 1940. Tommy Dorsey and his Orchestra were headlining, featuring an up-and-coming young singer named Frank Sinatra. Over the next twenty years, the stage featured acts including Glenn Miller, Harry James, Rosemary Clooney, Woody Herman, Peggy Lee, Lawrence Welk, and the Andrews Sisters. The Lawrence Welk Orchestra had previously spent five years playing the Aragon Ballroom on Santa Monica Pier. Aired on a local television station, Welk's shows did so well that ABC agreed to broadcast his show nationally. In need of a bigger venue, the first broadcast was live from the Hollywood Palladium, where the orchestra continued to play every Saturday night for years.

As the popularity of big-band music faded, the Palladium became a favorite venue for Latin music including stars such as Ray Vasquez and the Tito Puente Orchestra. In the late 1960s, acts from Jimi Hendrix, the Grateful Dead, Alice Cooper, the Doors, David Bowie, to Bob Marley were booking the venue. In 1971, the Grammy Awards show was televised for the first time from the Hollywood Palladium, which continued to be a popular music venue during the 1980s and '90s, but a series of near-riots in and around the venue caused the city to revoke its liquor license. For the next decade, the venue was only available for private events. Then the owners signed a long-term lease with Live Nation to book concerts. On October 15, 2008, Jay-Z took the stage and the Hollywood Palladium was once again open for business.

The Sky Room

TEL. L.B. 7-2201
FOR RESERVATIONS
THE NEW
Wilton Hotel
SKY ROOM
LONG BEACH, CALIF.

THE SKY ROOM · WILTON HOTEL · LONG BEACH · CALIF.

SKY ROOM
EL CORTEZ HOTEL
SAN DIEGO

TOP OF THE TOWN

EL CORTEZ HOTEL
Sky Room
SAN DIEGO, CALIF.

On June 22, 1926, the Sacramento Benevolent and Protective Order of Elks Lodge No. 6 cut the ribbon on its brand new temple. The fourteen-story building had nearly a hundred hotel rooms, stores on the ground floor, and a restaurant on the top level. **Top of the Town**'s cocktail lounge was known for its amazing view. In 1959, radio station KXRQ began to broadcast from its new studios on the thirteenth floor. At the time, it played a mixture of popular music and jazz. Then in 1968, a new owner decided to adapt a "freeform" radio format. A few months later, the newly christened KZAP made its debut as a rock 'n' roll station. It was an immediate hit and gained some notoriety when it was the first American radio station to air a commercial for condoms. Meanwhile, Elks Lodge No. 6 was not doing as well. In 1972, decreasing memberships forced the fraternal organization to sell the building. Top of the Town closed soon after, and KZAP moved its broadcast studio to another site.

Sky Room

ABOVE ALL IN HOLLYWOOD

ROOM AT THE TOP

D AIR TERMINAL ★ BURBANK, CALIFORNIA

Top OF THE Town
OPEN TO THE PUBLIC
COCKTAIL LOUNGE
RESTAURANT
ELKS
TEMPLE
11TH
J–STREET
SACRAMENTO
CALIFORNIA

TOP OF THE MARK

TOP OF THE MARK

HOTEL MARK HOPKINS
San Francisco

TOP OF THE MARK
HOTEL
Mark Hopkins
SAN FRANCISCO

LD FAMED

Top of the Mark

HOTEL MARK HOPKINS
NOB HILL • SAN FRANCISCO

"Top of the Mark"
World's most spectacular
Cocktail, Lounge
Mark Hopkins Hotel, San Francisco

GOLDEN GATE VIEWS

In 1906, when an earthquake nearly destroyed the city of San Francisco, only one hotel managed to survive the disaster: Hotel Majestic, which had opened in 1902, making it the Bay Area's oldest operating hotel. Other hotels quickly rebuilt and reopened. Those hotels are famous not only for their history, but for having some of the rooftop bars with the coolest views in the state. On a clear night, some imbibers can see all the way from the Golden Gate to San Jose.

Both tourists and locals visit the Mark Hopkins and take in the views from its **Top of the Mark** bar. The Empire Hotel was famous for its **Empire Sky Room**, as well as being featured in Alfred Hitchcock's classic film *Vertigo*. It's since become a boutique destination that's been renamed the Vertigo Hotel. The Sir Francis Drake on Union Square had not just one, but four noteworthy bars: the **Starlite Roof**, Golden Hind, Persian Room, and Drake's Tavern.

THE Sir Francis Drake
Starlite Roof

"Here's Stars in Your Eyes"
Starlite Roof
HOTEL SIR FRANCIS DRAKE
San Francisco

STARLIGHT ROOF
GOLDEN HIND
DRAKE'S TAVERN
HOTEL SIR FRANCIS DRAKE · SAN FRANCISCO

Empire SKY ROOM

DRINKING HABITS of the AMERICAN MALE

DRINK HEARTY BOYS!

A History of Cocktail Napkins

In the 1940s, paper was Wisconsin's third largest industry. Some companies such as Wisconsin Tissue Mills and Beach Products specialized in paper plates, cups, and cocktail napkins. Their salesmen visited bars and restaurants offering samples printed with various art and text. Humorous cartoons, usually related to alcohol, were especially popular. Customers could pay extra if they wanted the name of their establishments printed on the napkins. By the late 1950s, cocktail napkins were so popular that boxed sets were sold in stores. Finally! Middle America could throw a cocktail party at home.

Duke's
COCKTAILS
SAN BERNARDINO
COLTON, CALIF.

ARTHUR'S
COCKTAILS
799 LA CADENA
COLTON, CALIFORNIA

San Jose

DRINKING IN HISTORY

The original **Lou's Village** opened in 1946 and was a San Jose institution until it closed in 2005. Celebrities including Lucille Ball, Walt Disney, and California's Governor "Pat" Brown were regular diners. The place was also known for its live entertainment, acts that ranged from the Ink Spots to Scatman Crothers to comedian Lenny Bruce. But perhaps the most unusual performer to grace its stage was Maxine Holman with her "Educated Wolf."

Holman's act originated in vaudeville and was known as a 'Half and Half,' a performer who utilizes a vertically divided costume as well as hair and makeup to create the illusion of two people. The most common version would be a woman also dressed as a man, but there were variations of the traditional approach: devil and angel, savage and virgin, bride and groom. Maxine Holman donned a prop wolf head attached to her shoulders. She and the "wolf" danced to live music.

your
HOST

Lou's Village
RESTAURANT &
COCKTAIL LOUNGE

LUNCHEON AND DINNERS
OUTSIDE CATERING

1465 W. SAN CARLOS ST.
SAN JOSE, CALIF.
CY 3-4570

for your pleasure

Eating and Drinking

Two Four Si

CLUB
Tabu

AL C. KEARNEY · TROY HUDSON
So. First St. · San Jose, Calif.

Lou Lenny's
Bachelor's

SWING & JAZZ
RHYTHM & BLUES

Phone
CY 3-9756

26th and East Santa Clara Street · San Jose, California

Visit The Latest Club
1481 Almaden Rd.

Frank Americh's Oyster Loaf
WILLARD 187
SAN JOSE, CALIF. · 517 SANTA CLARA ST.

★ CLUB DANZABAR
★ DINING ROOMS
★ COFFEE SHOP
★ TAP ROOM

hotel
DE ANZA
SAN JOSE'S Newest
EL CAMINO REAL, SAN JOSE, CALIFORNIA

ing CORN
RAMI Sa

LUNCHEO
DRA
Fair Sho
2801 STEVENS

CHINESE FOOD

Sapphire

San Jose's Most BEAUTIFUL
Cocktail Lounge

UNSURPASSED FOR
FINE DRINKS

THE ATTIC

1347 McKEE ROAD, SAN JOSE

el Capitan

hotel DeANZA
SAN JOSE

Cocktails with a Personality

Tonic Room

992 EL CAMINO REAL
SUNNYVALE, CALIFORNIA
•
1897 ALUM ROCK AVE.
SAN JOSE, CALIFORNIA
•
2108 FREMONT BLVD.
MONTEREY, CALIFORNIA

STAGNARO'S
ARCADIA

COCKTAIL LOUNGE
and
RESTAURANT

Joe. J. Stagnaro
180 W. SAN CARLOS, ST.
SAN JOSE,
CALIF.

CATERING TO PRIVATE PARTIES
PHONE CHerry 3-7200

CABLE CAR
RESTAURANT

O'FARRELL, JONES
& HYDE STREETS

VALLEY
FAIR
SAN JOSE

CLOSE COVER BEFORE STRIKING

1300 SOUTH BASCOM AVE.
SAN JOSE, CALIFORNIA

Dick's
DRAGON 爵龍

V is for Victory

3 DOTS & A DASH

Donn Beach, founder of Don the Beachcomber, served as a lieutenant colonel in the Army Air Force during World War II. He was awarded a Purple Heart after being injured in a U-boat attack. When he recovered, the Army put him in charge of the Officer's Rest-and-Recreation Center program. During this time, he created some of his signature drinks like the Q.B. Cooler and the Test Pilot. To celebrate the war's end, he invented the 3 Dots & A Dash. In Morse code, three dots and a dash means "victory." Beach's famed drink has three cherries as dots and a dash made of pineapple.

GIN & TONIC

In the 1700s, gin was super popular with the masses in England. It was cheap to make, and even the poor who inhabited London's slums could afford it. Gin eventually made its way from the British Colonies across the continents to India. British soldiers stationed there were under constant threat of catching malaria. The only thing that could defend against the mosquito-borne disease was quinine powder, extracted from the bark of the cinchona tree. In 1858, businessman Erasmus Bond produced a commercially available elixir called "aerated tonic liquid" that was rich with quinine, but tasted so bitter it was hard to take. Clever soldiers began mixing it with sugar, lime juice, and gin, which led to the creation of the now-classic gin and tonic.

KEEP 'EM FLYING

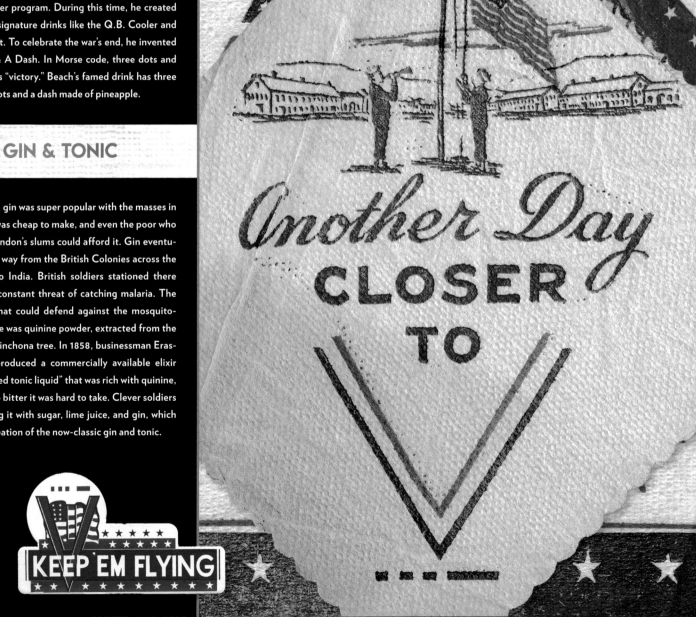

WE'RE ALL-AMERICANS!

41

GOD BLESS AMERICA!

Lee's Cocktail Lounge
189 S. FIRST ST.
SAN JOSE, CALIF.
J. B. Lee
—Prop.—

DRINK
and be
MERRY

A Girl in every Port

National Cafe

COCKTAILS
8947 NATIONAL BLVD.
LOS ANGELES, CALIFORNIA
VE 8-9541

FRENCH 75

The French 75 came about during World War I, though its specific origins are a little hazy. One version has flying ace Raoul Lufbery creating the drink. Most of his fellow aviators drank Champagne before a mission. Lufbery wanted something with a bit more kick, so he added cognac. But the drink is generally credited to barman Harry MacElhone at the New York Bar in Paris. His version was a mix of gin, Champagne, lemon juice, and sugar. Some years later, he bought the business and renamed it Harry's New York Bar. Harry's is still open, the French 75 is still on the menu, but nowadays they add a few drops of absinthe for that extra kick.

SUFFERING BASTARD

In 1942, World War II was raging in Africa between the British Army and Hitler's Afrika Korps under the command of Field Marshal Erwin Rommel. The Germans were close to securing the Suez Canal, which would have split the British Empire. Rommel was quoted as saying "I'll be drinking Champagne in the master suite at Shepheard's soon." Joe Scialom was the head bartender at the famous Cairo hotel. Because it was difficult to bring in proper supplies, Joe was forced to use cheap liquor. British officers complained about having terrible hangovers as a result. Endeavoring to create a drink that would prove more agreeable the next morning, Joe combined bourbon and gin with lime, ginger beer, and bitters. The result came to be known as the Suffering Bastard. His creation was so successful, he received a telegram from British High Command requesting that eight gallons be sent to the front lines at El-Alamein. The battle was a stalemate, but when Lt. General Montgomery took over, the British eventually pushed the Germans out of Africa.

Va-Va Voom!

GIRLS WHO WEAR GLASSES

The iconic image of a nude woman reclining in a cocktail glass has been around since the turn of the century. Vintage Champagne ads from France had flapper girls in oversized glasses surrounded by bubbles. In 1930, photographer Howard Redell took a black-and-white photo of a nude woman smoking a cigarette in a stemmed glass. The original image is on display at the Metropolitan Museum of Art in New York. In the 1964 comedy *What A Way to Go*, stars Shirley MacLaine and Robert Mitchum spend the night sleeping under pink silk sheets inside a bed-sized glass. In the twenty-first century, burlesque performer Dita Von Teese featured a giant champagne glass in her stage performances. And in the video for her hit song "Naughty Girl," Beyoncé gets downright sultry in a giant glass of bubbly.

Relax!

You're among friends!

LOS ANGELES

DINE & DANCE

HALF-WAY HOUSE
KINGSBURG, CALIFORNIA

SAN FRANCISCO

YOUR HOST-PETE TROISI

NAPOLI CAFE
ITALIAN & AMERICAN FOOD

PRIVATE PARTIES ONLY
WEDDINGS BANQUETS

CARMEN CITRIGNO, PROP.

950 So. 1st St. San Jose
For Reservations Call
CY. 5-9967

THE PINK PUSSYCAT

In the late 1950s, Harry Schiller opened the Club Seville in West Hollywood, but business was slow. Harry decided burlesque was the wave of the future. His wife Alice reluctantly went along with the idea, but she insisted that theirs would be a classy supper club. Alice came up with the name **Pink Pussycat** and had the building painted pink. She even acted as the club's hostess, greeting female patrons with a pink feather, and invented stage names for the dancers based on popular celebrities. Marquee headliners had names like Fran Sinatra, Samya Davis Jr., Deena Martin, and Peeler Lawford. Ironically, the real Rat Pack occasionally dropped by to take in the show. But it was the club's daytime activities that put the Pink Pussycat in the pages of *Time Magazine*.

The Schillers ran a striptease school where young ladies could learn, as the school flyer so demurely put it, the "Fundamentals of Taking It Off." Interested applicants had to be over age twenty-one, be of high moral character, show a serious interest in the art of striptease, and possess a voluptuous figure. The Schillers hired Sally Marr, a former burlesque star to teach the basics. Marr had also been a stand-up comedian, a talent she passed on to her famous son, Lenny Bruce, who would occasionally perform sets at the club. The Pink Pussycat folded in the late 1970s, and Harry Schiller turned the venue into a lesbian dance club called Peanuts.

Bakersfield

During the late 1950s and early 1960s, local musicians such as Buck Owens and Merle Haggard developed their own style that came to be known as the Bakersfield Sound. Visitors to Bakersfield can still get a taste of those classic sounds at renowned venues such as Buck Owens's Crystal Palace and the Old Corral Café. There's also live music at the Pyrenees Café, which has been serving Basque specialties like Oxtail Stew and Lamb Shank since 1901. The **Silver Fox Starlight Lounge** or Guthrie's Alley Cat also keep the Bakersfield spirit alive. Along with its iconic neon sign, Guthrie's Alley Cat is also famous for its unusual wallpaper.

In the mid 1950s, celebrated artist Al Hirschfeld created a large-scale line drawing of a Hollywood cocktail party. The guests included caricatures of stars like W.C. Fields, Laurel & Hardy, Marlene Dietrich, Pablo Picasso, and Joan Crawford. The artwork was made available as a limited-edition silk-screened wallpaper. There are only a handful of the Al Hirschfeld wallpaper panels still in existence. One of them is at Guthrie's Alley Cat, and another is in the Frolic Room, found at the corner of Hollywood and Vine

BLIND
ER BOWL
FIELD

The Ritz

Meet me at *The Ritz*
1810 EYE STREET
BAKERSFIELD, CALIF.

Maison-Jaussaud
FRENCH RESTAURANT

1001 S. UNION AVE.
BAKERSFIELD
CALIF.

COCKTAIL
LOUNGE

BAKERSFIELD INN

BAKERSFIELD
CALIFORNIA

Rancho
Bakersfield

U. S. 99 — NORTH OF CIRCLE

Looking Back

THE WILD WEST, GAY '90s, AND ROARING '20s

There's a good chance if you've spent any time in Anaheim, Orlando, or Branson, you've eaten at a theme restaurant. That meal probably involved massive hamburgers, multicolored drinks, and an opportunity to take a photo with a performer dressed in a costume (bonus points if the photo op also included a puppet or the server was speaking with a bad British accent). Theme restaurants were all the rage in the 1980s and '90s. It seemed like every tourist destination in the world had a Hard Rock Café or a Planet Hollywood, which were soon followed by other celebrity tie-in restaurants. The Fashion Café sponsored by Naomi Campbell, Claudia Schiffer, and Elle MacPherson. Andre Agassi, Wayne Gretsky, and Monica Seles promoted the All-Stars Cafe. By the time you get to the ESPN Café, Billboard Live, and the NASCAR Café, it's hard to believe there are more, but there's still Hooters.

There's no simple definition of a "theme restaurant." It's not just the décor or a menu geared to a certain type of food. A British pub can proudly fly the Union Jack and serve fish and chips, but that doesn't make it a theme restaurant. However, if that same pub claims to be an exact recreation of Jack the Ripper's favorite Whitechapel watering hole, complete with souvenir T-shirt, then it's a theme restaurant.

For better or for worse, theme restaurants create an environment that people might not be able to experience otherwise. That could be the jungles of Brazil at the Rainforest Café or the chance to make lemonade out of lemons at Bubba Gump's Shrimp Company. The concept has been around for more than a century. A trio of cabaret clubs opened in Montmartre, the red-light district of Paris, in the late 1800s. Rather than Gibson guitars or Brazilian jungles, they each used death as the theme. Cabaret du Neant (Cabaret of Nothingness) treated its patrons like freshly buried cadavers. Waiters dressed as pallbearers, coffins

STOVE PIPE WELLS VILLAGE

DEATH VALLEY CALIFORNIA

"Amidst California's Magnificent Redwoods"

LA HONDA, CALIF.

Boots and Saddle Lodge

"Where There's Fun for One
There's Fun for All"

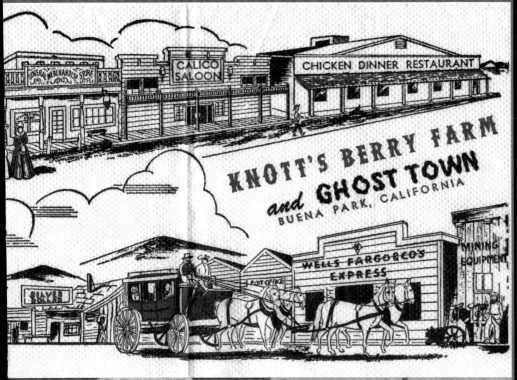

CALICO SALOON

CHICKEN DINNER RESTAURANT

GENERAL MERCHANDISE STORE

KNOTT'S BERRY FARM and GHOST TOWN
BUENA PARK, CALIFORNIA

WELLS FARGO&CO'S EXPRESS

POST OFFICE

MINING EQUIPMENT

SILVER

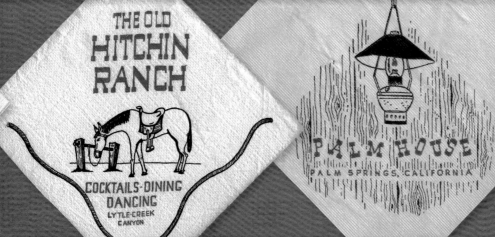

THE OLD HITCHIN RANCH

COCKTAILS·DINING DANCING
LYTLE·CREEK CANYON

PALM HOUSE
PALM SPRINGS, CALIFORNIA

substituted for tables, and a chandelier built with bones hung overhead. Wine was served in artificial skulls and a lucky volunteer would be transformed into a skeleton, an effect achieved with a Pepper's Ghost hologram. At Cabaret de L'Enfer (Cabaret of Hell), the façade was a giant demonic mouth and a doorman who greeted customers shouting "Enter and be damned." Waiters inside dressed like devils, and a small band played selections from the opera *Faust* by Charles Gounod.

If guests didn't want to end their night damned to Purgatory, they could go next door to Cabaret du Ciel (Cabaret of the Sky), where waiters dressed as angels, and the entertainment included a visit from St. Peter who blessed bar patrons with holy water. Café du Bagne (Café of the Penitentiary) was a little more down-to-earth. Diners ate in a room resembling a prison eating hall with waiters dressed as convicts dragging around balls and chains.

The concept made its way across the Atlantic in 1896 when the Cabaret du Neant sponsored performances in New York City. Then, Don Dickerman opened the Pirate's Den in Greenwich Village, which was so popular that he opened other branches, including one in Los Angeles. Servers staged mock battles and female patrons were held in the brig until they screamed, which entitled them to something called a Scream Diploma.

Times changed and theme restaurants began to appeal more to families. Country-Western chains included the Longhorn Steakhouse, Red Barn, and Nickerson Farms, which served burgers and steaks amid hay bales and cowboy memorabilia. San Francisco's Barbary Coast was a big influence on places like Victoria Station and the beloved ice cream parlor chain Farrell's, where kids devoured banana splits right along with mom and dad.

THE GREEN SPOT MOTEL

In 2020, Netflix released the David Fincher film *Mank* starring Gary Oldman as screenwriter Herman Mankiewicz. The Oscar-nominated production is the story of how Mank created the script for the 1941 classic, *Citizen Kane*. The film's director and star, Orson Welles, was facing a tight deadline. Knowing that his screenwriter was a notorious alcoholic, he banished Mankiewicz to Verde Ranch in Victorville, far from the temptations of Hollywood. Welles also arranged to have his long-time collaborator John Houseman keep an eye on Mank and the script. At the end of each day, the writer was allowed one drink. Mank and Houseman would drive into town and have that drink at the **Green Spot Café**, adjacent to the Green Spot Motel. In just over a month, a sprawling 270-page first draft titled *American* was sent to Welles who used it as a basis for *Citizen Kane*. Welles and Mank shared screenwriting credit, as well as the Oscar for their screenplay.

Herman Mankiewicz died of uremic poisoning in 1953. Verde Ranch became Kemper Campbell Ranch, and Fincher filmed *Mank*'s exterior scenes there. The Green Spot Café burned down in a fire in 1954, but the motel is still open on Route 66.

The Barbary Coast was a red-light district in San Francisco that emerged during the 1849 Gold Rush. Prospectors were pouring into the city looking to strike it rich. If they were lonely, bored, or homesick, the Barbary Coast provided nine blocks of saloons, dance halls, and bordellos to cheer them up. Most of that was destroyed in the 1906 earthquake, and whatever was left was done-in by Prohibition.

But the Barbary Coast's spirit was kept alive a few blocks away in North Beach. In the 1950s and '60s, it was the home for clubs like Basin Street West, Mr. D's, the Hungry i, and Ann's Nightclub, where comedian Lenny Bruce got his start.

Around that same time, high-end restaurants like Goman's Gay '90s, Ernie's, and the Ritz Old Poodle Dog were embracing the Victorian ambiance of the red-light bordellos. But with one Bay Area restaurant, it was more than just a recreation.

Sally Stanford eloped when she was sixteen and before she was even twenty-one, she had spent two years in prison and opened a brothel in the Tenderloin District. By the time she was thirty-seven, she was the madam of a bordello on Nob Hill frequented by politicians and celebrities including Errol Flynn and Humphrey Bogart. In 1949, she opened a restaurant in Sausalito, **Sally Stanford's Valhalla**. Sally claimed to have "gone legit," but the red light above the backdoor said otherwise. City officials tried to close down her place by pulling her liquor license.

Sally decided to fight back and ran for city council. It took five tries, but she won the seat. Once in office, her popularity led to her being elected mayor in 1976. She retired after one term, but the council officially named her "Vice Mayor For Life."

Sally passed away in 1982, and Valhalla closed a few years later. The town erected a life-sized statue of the former madam-turned-mayor and a fountain at the ferry landing reads "Have a drink on Sally."

GAY 90's

ON RESTAURANT ROW
BEVERLY HILLS

"Coman's Gay 90's Please"

345 BROADWAY · SAN FRANCISCO

Coach Room

1101 E. Huntington Dr.
MONROVIA. ELLIOTT 8-9241

PLANTATION

Cocktail Lounge

VIRGINIA RECREATION
CENTER
25 CHESTNUT PLACE
LONG BEACH
CALIF.

CARMEL · BY · THE · SEA
CALIFORNIA

PINE INN
COCKTAIL PARLOR

the
NOB H
restaur
RANDRAMA

THE ROARING '20s

In the mid 1950s, businessman Paul Cummins opened his first restaurant, a coffee shop called Huddle. Cummins went on to open fifteen branches in the Huddle chain, followed by a number of steakhouses called Eaton's. Eager to try something different, he and a partner opened the Gay '90s restaurant on La Cienega. It was billed as "A Saloon Created For The Carriage Trade" and brought to Los Angeles the Barbary Coast aesthetic so popular in San Francisco. His next venture was Sports Page next door to the Gay '90s. Today, sports bars are commonplace. But in the mid 1950s, the concept was only popular with local athletes and sportswriters.

Eventually, Cummins sold his share of the Gay '90s and converted the Sports Page into **Paul Cummins Roaring 20's**. A monument to indulgent excess with eight different rooms, each offering its own brand of live entertainment. Local advertisements promised the following:

> Two mad swinging Dixieland bands, six great pianos, the grand march of 30 beautiful Roaring 20's girls—right across the bar top. Flappers swinging from the ceiling and sliding down the shoot-the-chutes! Silent flickers and free Charleston lessons. All that Jazz and Razzmatazz! Live it all over again!

Aloha!

TIKI BAR CULTURE

The Māori are the indigenous people of mainland New Zealand. In their mythology, Tiki was the first man and Marikoriko was the first woman. The wood or stone carving the Māori make of these early human figures became known as a *tiki*. Different island cultures have their own names for the icons. In Hawaii, they're known as *Ki'i*. These carvings often mark the boundaries of sacred sites and represent deified ancestors.

So, how did something with such spiritual origins lead to a culture defined by flaming rum cocktails, Hawaiian shirts, and *Gilligan's Island*? Two answers: Donn Beach and Victor Bergeron.

Ernest Raymond Beaumont Gantt was born in Limestone County, Texas, on February 22, 1907. At twenty, he left home to travel the world. His restless nature led him to Australia, then to the South Pacific, where he found a mystic paradise of sunset beaches and rum-soaked palm trees. He returned to the states and settled in Los Angeles just in time for an auspicious event: the end of Prohibition. For thirteen years, men and women had been forced to drink homemade hooch in overpriced speakeasies and back-alley gin joints. It was the Jazz Age, and a thirsty nation was ready to go on a bender.

Sensing an opportunity, Gantt rented a tiny twenty-five-seat bar in Hollywood and filled it with nautical knick-knacks he had collected in his travels. **Don's Beachcomber** was born after he legally changed his name to Donn Beach. A one-time bootlegger, he created his own unique rum-based drinks which he called Rhum Rhapsodies—luscious libations that conjured images of tropical indulgence. Sumatra Kula, Cobra's Fang, Tahitian Rum Punch, Navy Grog. But none were as famous—or infamous—as his signature zombie, what he called "a mender of broken dreams." Bartenders were only allowed to serve two zombies per customer. The bar was a post-prohibition hit. Don the

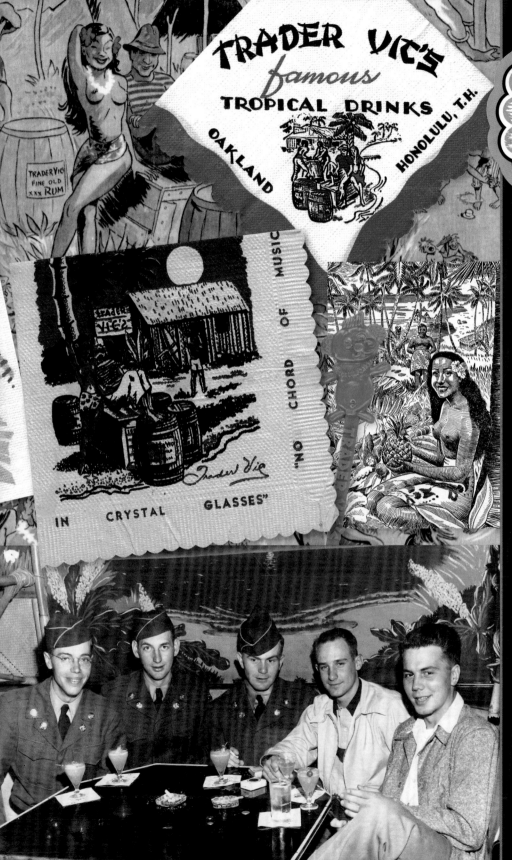

hit. Don the Beachcomber, and the tiki bar culture as we know it was officially born.

Beach's success soon inspired a variety of imitators. Some were cheap knock-offs, but others were equally as lush, exotic, and successful, and none more so than **Trader Vic's**. Victor Bergeron was raised in Oakland, California, and despite losing a leg to tuberculosis, he said he had a happy childhood. Years later, he would tell anyone who asked that a hungry shark bit off his leg. In 1934, he opened Hinky Dink's, a fun spot known for its low prices on "Booze and Chow." Business boomed and Bergeron was inspired by places he visited: the Bon Ton Bar in New Orleans, Floridita in Havana, and especially Don the Beachcomber.

Hinky Dink's re-emerged as a tiki bar, complete with lava rocks and totem poles, plus signature cocktails including the Fog Cutter and the Scorpion Bowl. He got credit for inventing the mai tai, though Beach claimed that was a knockoff of his own Q.B. Cooler. Nobody cared (except maybe Beach), and the mai tai became the iconic tiki cocktail.

Exotic South Seas restaurants and bars began to open across the state: **Zombie Village** in Oakland, Mermaid Room in Millbrae, Leilani Hut in Long Beach, and the South Seas Café in San Diego. An idea that was born in a tiny twenty-five-seat bar was now a part of the national culture. Ironically, the man who started it all sold control of Don the Beachcomber to his exwife and moved to Hawaii. Donn Beach then opened a new restaurant called Waikiki Village which featured nightly music sets by tiki icon Martin Denny and a myna bird trained to shout "Give me a beer, stupid." Apparently, myna birds don't drink mai tais.

117

SOUTH SEAS CLUB

Businesswoman Vivian Laird opened her first nightclub, Garden of Allah, in 1933, and its success led to three more venues: the Bohemia Lounge, Brass Rail, and **South Seas** in Anaheim. Advertisements for the South Seas promised an exotic Hawaiian atmosphere and delicious dinners prepared by female chefs. That changed when Herb Ward took over. Under his management, the only women working at the club were stripping nightly on stage. The clientele was so rough, the manager paid the police to have a special deputy on site on busy nights. One dancer with the stage name of "Dimples" Morgan was arrested for her fig-leaf dance. According to the arresting officers, the fig leaf wasn't big enough, and that she "exposed her person to the view of the noisy crowd."

7 SEAS RESTAURANT

Ray Haller opened the **7 Seas Restaurant** on Hollywood Boulevard directly across from Grauman's Chinese Theatre. Along with the prerequisite Polynesian décor, there were nightly tropical storms created by spraying water on a corrugated tin roof along with thunder and lightning effects. When businessman Bob Brooks took over, he added a tropical floor show. But the club fell on hard times and by the late 1980s, Hollywood locals were calling it "The 7 Sleaze."

Bob Brooks'
7 - SEAS

RESTAURANT

6904 HOLLYWOOD BLVD.

HOLLYWOOD
CALIF.

CANTONESE &
AMERICAN MENUS

Phone HO. 5-6761

6904 Hollywood Blvd., Hollywood, Calif.

Bob Brooks'
7 SEAS

DANCING & DINING

115 EAST 5th STREET · OXNARD, CALIFORNIA

Hody's Garden Rm.

PACIFIC COAST HIGHWAY & ANAHEIM BLVD.
LONG BEACH

Dinners   Luncheons

South Seas Cafe   Shrimp   3877 Pacific Hiway
"RAIN ON THE ROOF"   Lobster   San Diego, Calif.
Sizzling Steaks   Country Fried Chicken
All Food   Cooked to Order

CY. 5-1606

CAUTION
ADULTS
AT
PLAY

ZAMBOANGA SOUTH SEA NITE CLUB

The **Zamboanga South Sea Nite Club** got its unusual name from the city of Zamboanga in the Philippines. The club's signature drink was a rum cocktail called the Tailless Monkey. Most likely, this was inspired by the song "The Monkeys Have No Tails in Zamboanga." Originally written in 1907, Abe Lyman had a minor hit when he recorded another version called "The Monkeys Have No Tails in Pago Pago."

The
WORLD'S
MOST BEAUTIFUL
POLYNESIAN PARADISE

3 FLOOR SHOWS
Every Nite
DINING DANCING

ZAMBOANGA
South Sea
Nite Club
3828 W. SLAUSON
LOS ANGELES, CALIF.
AX. 15114

HOME OF THE
TAILESS MONKEYS

OH, BOY!
MEET ME AT
ZAMBOANGA!

caribbean lounge

MINNIE'S
COCKTAILS
DINING
MODESTO, CALIFORNIA

JAVA-TIME
SANTA MONICA
IN THE HORACE HEIDT ARCADE
COCKTAILS ...... FINE FOOD

LANAI
San Mateo
California

RONTIKI
COCKTAILS
Redwood City, Calif.

DID YOU KNOW
THAT ON THE
ISLAND OF ZAMBOANGA
THERE IS A TRIBE OF MEN THAT
HAVE TAILS ABOUT 6 INCHES LONG?

THE MONKEYS
HAVE NO TAILS
IN
ZAMBOANGA!
So
FOR AN EVENING
OF THE FINEST
& MOST UNUSUAL
ENTERTAINMENT
Visit

ZAMBOANGA
South Sea Nite Club
3828 W. SLAUSON

121

TONGA ROOM

The Fairmont Hotel is one of San Francisco's oldest and most luxurious hotels. It's also one of the city's most popular places for a cocktail. At one time, the Nob Hill hotel had five different hot spots for drinking and dancing the night away: Venetian Room, where Tony Bennett first sang "I Left My Heart in San Francisco" in December 1961; Papagayo Room, which boasted of its "Mexican Atmosphere;" La Ronde Room which had a working carousel with a bar in the center; Cirque Room, and the renowned **Tonga Room**. Only Tonga Room survives, and it hasn't changed much since it opened in 1945. A Top 40 band plays on a floating barge in a lagoon that was once the hotel's pool. Tropical storms blow through every thirty minutes, and the Pupu Platter is still served along with the hotel's mai tai and signature Fog Cutter.

Gene's **Hawaiian Village**

10637 SO. VERMONT   LOS ANGELES, CALIF.

Tonga Room

FAIRMONT HOTEL
SAN FRANCISCO

Fairmont
HOTEL
ATOP NOB HILL · SAN FRANCISCO · CALIFORNIA
Home of the
VENETIAN ROOM ★ CAMELLIA ROOM
CIRQUE ROOM ★ LA RONDE BAR
SQUIRE ROOM ★ TONGA ROOM
COFFEE ROOM ★ BLUM'S
PAPAGAYO ROOM

PAGAN IDOL
375 BUSH STREET SAN FRANCISCO

CIRQUE ROOM
COCKTAILS - DANCING

TONGA ROOM
CHINESE-AMERICAN FOOD

Venetian Room
DINNER DANCING

PAPAGAYO ROOM
MEXICAN ATMOSPHERE

Camellia Room
DINING

La Ronde Room
EXCITING
COCKTAIL LOUNGE

Fabulous
Fairmont Hotel
ATOP NOB HILL - SAN FRANCISCO

BALi HA'i
Shelter Island
POINT LOMA
SAN DIEGO,
CALIF.

122

Last Call!

Some things haven't changed since the end of Prohibition. If you order a drink, the bartender will still set your glass on a cocktail napkin. But inevitably, it will be a square of plain white paper. There might be a logo on it, if you're drinking at a nice hotel. But the days of colorful graphics and bawdy innuendos are—for the most part— long past. Napkins like the ones seen on the pages of this book have become as rare as free matchbooks and souvenir swizzle sticks—ironic, since cocktails are more popular than ever. The Craft Cocktail Revolution that exploded in the 1990s is here to stay. Nearly 20,000 members of the liquor-and-service industry gather annually in New Orleans for a five-day conference known as "Tales of the Cocktail."

What these vintage napkins offer isn't just cool retro art and a few memories for anyone over fifty. Each one is a square paper snapshot of a way of life that's come and gone, a souvenir from a period in history as equally flawed as ours today. But perhaps it was the last time that we could find ways to make light of our flaws and weaknesses. It was a time when a stiff drink and the right song on the jukebox could make everything seem all right.

In the spring of 1958, when Frank Sinatra was in the studio recording the lyrics Johnny Mercer wrote down on that cocktail napkin fifteen years before, he was still nursing a broken heart over his shattered affair with Ava Gardner. Frank nailed the song in one take. It was his Valentine to all the broken promises ever scrawled on a cocktail napkin and sealed with a lipstick kiss.

Acknowledgments

Stephen King once wrote "Writing is a lonely job. Having someone who believes in you makes a lot of difference." Fortunately, my wife Christel has always believed in me and my work. She is my best friend, occasional editor, and constant travel companion—so I raise a glass in loving thanks to her.

Thanks, too, to my publisher Paddy Calistro who guided me along the path of publishing my first book, to my editor Terri Accomazzo, and to everyone else at Angel City Press. A double-shot shoutout to graphic artist J. Eric Lynxwiler, who not only created the amazing design of this book, but also contributed napkins and photos from his own private collection.

Lastly, a toast to all the vendors at swap meets and on eBay who helped me build this collection—especially Randy Jones who sold me my first napkin collection at the Pasadena City College Flea Market back in 2017. Who knew that a box of vintage cocktail napkins would lead to this.

About the Author and Designer

A longtime Angeleno, **Patrick Quinn** works as a production designer at Universal Studios in Hollywood. He and his wife spend most weekends at swap meets and antique malls, searching for treasures. This allows him to indulge in an ever-growing collection of vintage odds 'n' ends, including lounge music LPs, 1970s snapshots, Western Union telegrams, early travel guides, and, of course, cocktail napkins.

As a Los Angeles cultural historian, **J. Eric Lynxwiler** has examined his favorite city as a co-author and designer for multiple Angel City Press books on Southern California topics, including *Wilshire Boulevard*, *Knott's Berry Farm*, *Spectacular Illumination*, and *Bunker Hill*. He is the popular host of Neon Cruises for the Museum of Neon Art and hits flea markets for vintage photos and paper ephemera.

Bar Keeps: A Collection of California's Best Cocktail Napkins

By Patrick Quinn

Copyright © 2022 Patrick Quinn. All rights reserved.

Design by J. Eric Lynxwiler, Signpost Graphics

10 9 8 7 6 5 4 3 2 1

ISBN-13 978-1-62640-097-9

Library of Congress Cataloging-in-Publication Data is available.

Published by Angel City Press
www.angelcitypress.com
Printed in Canada